THE BOBBSEY TWINS
IN A TV MYSTERY SHOW

When the Bobbsey twins fly to California to be in a television show, they have no idea they will find a mystery awaiting them.

During rehearsals, they befriend a beautiful, long-haired dog who has been specially trained for the show and discover a tiny key in his fur. Suddenly the dog disappears from the set without a trace. Everything is in a dither. Did he run away or was he stolen?

The twins are sure that the key is their first clue to the mystery. But what does it open? Their clever investigation and fearless persistence help them uncover the animal's secret and results in the capture of a ring of unscrupulous thieves whose work spreads far beyond the state of California.

"We look like monster twins!" Freddie bubbled.

The Bobbsey Twins In a TV Mystery Show

By

LAURA LEE HOPE

GROSSET & DUNLAP
A FILMWAYS COMPANY
Publishers • New York

PRINTED IN THE UNITED STATES OF AMERICA
LIBRARY OF CONGRESS CATALOG CARD NO. 77-76127
ISBN: 0-448-08071-0
The Bobbsey Twins in a TV Mystery Show

CONTENTS

The Bobbsey Twins
In a TV Mystery Show

CHAPTER 1

KEY QUESTION

"Smile! television mystery stars." commanded a young woman with long thick brown hair and sparkling brown eyes.

"Okay, Marcy!" Nan Bobbsey grinned. She posed in the glare of a spotlight next to her twin brother Bert. They were twelve and had dark hair and eyes.

"Don't forget us," piped up Flossie Bobbsey. She pulled her six-year-old blond twin Freddie in front of the older children.

"Oh, I wouldn't forget you," Marcy said. She aimed her camera at the foursome. "Say 'cheese.'"

"Woof!"

"Waldo wants to be in the picture too!" Flossie squealed as a large gray-and-white sheep dog trotted toward her.

"He always wants to get into the act," said the plump man behind him with a chuckle, "just like every other actor I know in California, except maybe you kids. But it doesn't take long."

"What doesn't take long?" Freddie asked.

"Getting to be a ham like Waldo," he said and opened a small wooden box filled with colorful lipsticks, powders, and make-up brushes.

"Waldo's not a ham." Flossie defended the dog as he sat beside her. "He's a nice sheep doggy."

She cuddled him and buried her face in his shaggy hair.

"Now, how is your chaperone P.R. lady—" the man began.

"P.R.?" Flossie repeated as she nuzzled Waldo.

"Public relations," he explained. "Well, how is Marcy going to take a picture of your big blue eyes, honey?"

"Like this," Flossie giggled and raised her head.

The man dipped into a cake of peach-colored powder and dabbed it on the little girl's nose.

"Perfect, Abe," Marcy said and clicked her camera.

Its sudden flash of light made Waldo bark. He leaped up quickly, overturning the make-up box, and knocking Flossie down.

"Waldo!" everyone cried as one paw slid into a pot of sticky orange rouge.

The dog skated past Freddie, who dived for the animal's collar and missed it, but he pulled out a clump of matted hair and landed next to his sister.

"What's this?" he asked, feeling something thin and hard in his hand.

Before he could examine it, Waldo had rolled between him and Flossie. He lay still and panted hard.

"Has our star pooch played enough for one day?" Abe said, cleaning up the mess of make-up on the floor.

Waldo did not reply.

"I have," said Freddie.

"Me too," added Flossie.

Freddie now pulled the clump of hair apart.

"Hey, look at what I found on Waldo!" he exclaimed. "It's a key!"

"A key?" Nan inquired.

"Let me see it," Bert said, taking it from his brother. "It's fairly small. It could be a key to a suitcase or a locker of some sort."

"Maybe Waldo carries his personal doghouse key," Marcy quipped.

"This is no ordinary dog, you know," said Abe. "He probably has his own swimming pool too!"

"I think it's strange to find a key stuck to a dog, don't you?" Bert asked Nan.

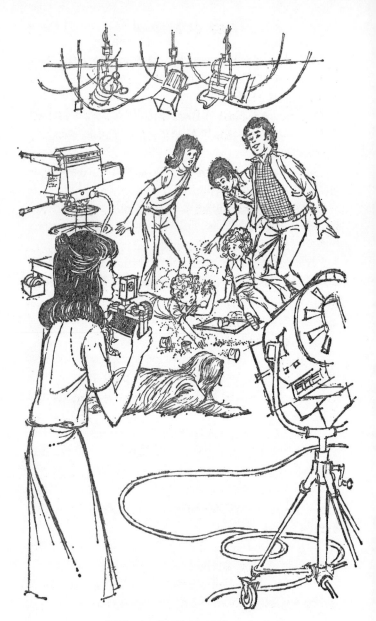

"What's this?" Freddie asked.

"I'd say it's a mystery," she answered. "And over there, 'The Mystery of the Hidden Caves' is about to begin."

"Come on, Nan," Bert said, "it's our scene."

"Hang on to this," Nan told Freddie, handing him the key.

Before Freddie could say a word, his older brother and sister had hurried toward a young freckle-faced man with a pencil stuck behind one ear.

"Mr. Little, are you ready for us yet?" Nan asked.

"Just about," he replied. "Considering you kids have never performed in front of a camera before, you're okay."

Nan blushed.

"I mean it. This is only the second day of film production, and you've learned the ropes as well as some actors who've been here at Globe Studios for years."

"Thanks," Bert said. "We were nervous when the studio auditioned us for this TV show, but everyone's been so nice. We feel at home."

Wayne Little smiled, then boomed. "Everybody on set now! We're going to have a quick rehearsal first. Come here, Waldo."

While Nan and Bert quickly scanned their scripts, the dog ambled toward them.

"I still can't believe we're really going to be on television," Nan whispered to Bert.

"Have you got the wet suits on?" Wayne interrupted the twins.

"Yes, but you'd never know it," said Nan.

She wore slacks and a sport blouse, which neatly covered her rubber suit underneath. Bert also had on slacks and a shirt.

"That water is cool, so the wet suits ought to keep you warm," Wayne said.

He glanced at the large metal pit in front of them with part of a cave tunnel in the middle of it. The pit was half-filled with water. A man wearing a full-length rubber suit helped Nan and Bert into the pit, then got out.

"Jay, you can start churning up that water now," Wayne called out to him.

"Okay."

The man immediately picked up a long T-shaped pole and stirred up the water.

"Harder," Wayne ordered.

"I'll help him," a second man on the film crew said, and fetched a similar pole. Soon the water was swirling and lapping against the side of the pit.

"Are you kids all right?" another man asked the Bobbseys.

"Fine, Mr. Kordel," Bert said.

"As director of this show, I order you to call me Kord." The tall slender man smiled.

Nan and Bert rehearsed the scene quickly, then returned to their starting point behind the cave.

"This is picture everybody. M.O.S. M.O.S.!" Wayne announced.

Nan nudged Bert. "What does that mean?" she whispered.

"Mit out sound. Shhh."

The crewman seated behind the camera on a crane was lowered over the pit toward the cave entrance from which Bert and Nan would emerge.

"Action!" the director said quietly.

Bert, in the lead, held a lantern high. "Be careful, Cindy. There are some sharp stones ahead. I just stubbed my toe on one."

The boy angled the light against the damp cave wall. "I wonder how far this cave goes," he continued.

"Maybe too far for us. Peter, let's go back!"

The chill of the water made Nan shiver a little but she knew that Cindy, the character she was playing, could not show it.

"This is no time to be chicken."

"I'm not chicken."

As the boy swung his lantern under the arched opening of the cave, he discovered an arrow crudely drawn on the wall. He fingered it.

"Look. This is fresh paint," he said.

"Maybe somebody is leading us into a trap."

The director of the scene now motioned Jay and his helper to stir up the water as hard as possible. It swirled rapidly through the pit, causing waves to foam and rise fiercely around the twins.

Fearful, Nan backed up, ready to leave the tunnel.

"Oh!" she cried, catching her foot on something in the floor of the pit.

She tumbled into the water. Bert dropped the lantern and tried to grab his sister's arm.

"Nan!" Bert cried, swallowing some water.

Waldo dashed between the cameraman and the director and flew into the pit, knocking Bert off balance and sending a shower of water over the entire crew.

"Cut!" the director ordered, spitting out a mouthful of spray. "Who's supposed to be watching that crazy animal? Slim Willis, where are you?"

A thin, wiry man in blue jeans jumped in after Waldo while Jay rescued the twins. Soon, with hair and clothes dripping wet, Nan and Bert approached John Kordel.

"I'm sorry, Kord," Nan coughed. "My foot got stuck on something."

"That's okay. We got most of it on film. Are you all right?"

"Mm-hmm."

"That's good. You just dry off now and relax. The wardrobe lady will take care of you."

Sylvia, a trim-figured woman with blonde hair swept back in a knot, wrapped a terrycloth towel around Nan's hair. She led her and Bert to a sunlamp standing next to a series of dressing tables. Freddie and Flossie scrambled toward them with Marcy close behind.

"What happened?" Marcy asked.

"I told you to watch out for those rocks," Bert teased his twin sister.

"You told Cindy, not me," Nan retorted. "I don't think the bottom of that pit is supposed to be really rocky."

"What do you mean?" Freddie inquired.

"Well, it should be rocky but it's only make-believe."

Meanwhile, Jay was examining the floor under the cave. Soon he surfaced, shaking his head in bewilderment.

"What did you find?" Wayne Little asked him.

"The floor is cracked and somebody tried to patch it with rocks. He did a bad job too."

Kord did not speak but motioned him out of the water. Freddie and Flossie edged near them.

"What do you mean 'somebody tried to patch it with rocks'?" Kord asked.

"Just what I said. That floor is concrete. It looks to me like somebody deliberately drilled across it. If it had cracked much more, the stage would have flooded out!"

CHAPTER II

WHERE'S WALDO?

"IF the stage flooded out—" Freddie started to say.

Flossie gasped.

What would have happened to Nan and Bert?

The young detectives ran to the older twins, who were by themselves now. They repeated what they had overheard.

"Why would anyone want to tamper with the floor of that pit?" Nan asked.

"I don't know," said Freddie.

"Me neither."

"There could be lots of reasons," Bert said. "Maybe there's something hidden under the floor. Maybe somebody wanted to do us in."

"Or maybe someone wanted to delay the show somehow," Nan suggested.

As she spoke, a giant electric pump was wheeled near the pit and hooked up to an opening at the bottom of it. The motor was switched on. Soon water was being sucked through a long hose that led out of the large stage doors and emptied on the pavement. The noise of the pump was deafening.

"It hurts my ears!" Flossie said, putting her hands over them.

"Let's go, Floss," Freddie said.

"Wait a second," their older sister interrupted. "Who's that?"

She pointed to a young boy and girl who were talking with John Kordel near the entrance to the sound stage. They had dark hair, almost black, and were about as tall as Nan and Bert. They looked very much alike.

"They could be you and me," Nan commented to her twin.

"As a matter of fact, they could play the roles of Cindy and Peter," he observed.

"Let's introduce ourselves."

The four Bobbseys walked toward the pair. They grimaced.

"I'm Nan Bobbsey," the older girl said pleasantly.

"Would you excuse us," the other one snapped. "We have some business with Mr. Kordel."

"Oh, I-I'm sorry."

"These are Caramel and Chester Potts," the director interjected. "They are—"

"Mr. Kordel," Chester cut him off. "We came to talk to you, not to them."

The director cleared his throat nervously while the Bobbseys excused themselves.

"Boy, are they weird!" Freddie whispered, out of earshot of the pair.

"Obviously, they don't like us very much," said Bert.

"What did we ever do to them?" Flossie said.

Nan shrugged. "Let me see that key again," she said to her younger brother.

He dug into his pocket. Then, feeling a hand on his shoulder, left the key where it was.

"Don't let those Potts kids bother you," Mr. Kordel said. "They were brought up by Grady, their older brother, after their parents died in a circus accident. He works for Globe Studios. You'll meet him soon."

"Why don't they like us?" Freddie asked.

"They don't dislike you."

"Well, they weren't very friendly," Bert remarked.

"Oh, they tested for the show you're in and seem to think they should have won the parts. Of course, every one of the fifty who tried out thought he or she should have been picked. They all had had some professional acting experience—"

"I was in a school play once," Flossie declared proudly. "I played Martha Washington."

"And I played George," added Freddie.

"To tell the truth, Freddie, we didn't choose you because of your acting credits. Since our TV show is about kids who solve a baffling mystery, we thought of the Bobbsey twins immediately. After all, why not use kids who solve real mysteries?"

"I think the TV story is a neat one," Nan said. "But I don't understand one thing."

"What's that?"

"Why don't you film all the scenes in sequence, from beginning to end?"

"Like the way you see it on television," Freddie added.

"Besides our show, there are about ten others being produced here at the studio. Now and then one of them needs to use the same sound stage or the same outside location. Aside from that, it's often more convenient to do several scenes that take place in the same location, one right after the other."

"So," Bert concluded, "if there are three scenes to do in the same living room, even though there's lots of other stuff to film in between, you try to do all the living-room scenes on the same day."

"More or less."

By now, the water pump had been turned off and Nan peered in the direction of the empty pit.

"Do you have any idea why someone would want to delay the production of this show?" she asked.

The director rubbed his chin with his finger.

"Now don't start looking for problems that don't exist," he said. "We've only got six days to finish this show. Every minute is precious to us and I don't want you to trouble yourselves over anything but your scripts."

"Do you know if anyone tried to keep us out of this show?" Bert questioned. He glanced at the crack in the floor of the pit. It was poorly lined with jagged rock.

"N-no, not really."

"Not really?" Flossie repeated.

"Well, some joker sent me a crazy letter last week. Said he was going to get even with the studio for not casting his children instead of you."

"Did he sign his name?" Freddie asked.

"Was there a return address? Did you notice the postmark on the envelope?" Nan went on.

"Slow down," Mr. Kordel said. "I threw it away. This isn't the first time somebody has gotten all steamed up because he or someone he knew lost out on a role. If I—"

The young detectives apologized for all the questioning.

"Now where's Slim Willis?" Mr. Kordel said, glancing at the crew.

Some of the men were moving lights from one

corner of the cave set to the other. The rest were swiveling the large crane with its camera to another position behind the cave.

"Slim?" the director called out again, as the skinny man bobbed up behind the crane. "We'll be ready for Waldo in two minutes."

His words were interrupted by the ring of a phone on a nearby wall. "Call for Marcy Sigler. Call for Miss Sigler," a voice announced.

She took the call, spoke briefly, then dashed up to the Bobbseys. "The studio wants me to photograph a guest star for another new show," she said, breathless. "Kord, what time do you expect to finish shooting today?"

"About four-thirty if there are no more minor catastrophes."

Marcy turned to the twins. "I should be back here by four. I'll take you to the hotel then. Okay? Bye."

No sooner had she left the building than Slim Willis nervously blurted out, "Waldo's gone!"

"Gone?" Mr. Kordel exclaimed. "This is no time to play games, Slim."

"I'm not playing games. He's gone. I can't find him." The man shifted nervously from one foot to another. "I don't know what to do. I-I can't figure out what could've happened to him—"

"Don't worry," Nan interrupted, as he wiped a wrinkle of perspiration from his face. "We'll try to find him."

"Waldo is gone!" Slim Willis declared.

"Oh, he's a smart one. Waldo's a really smart one," Slim repeated anxiously. "I—"

The man broke off speaking as Freddie and Bert ran outside.

"Waldo!" they chorused.

"You check out those sound stages," Bert said to his brother. He indicated a short row of big, block buildings with large numbers painted on them.

"Okay," Freddie replied and darted ahead.

He glanced between the buildings and paused by an open stage door. A man in a cowboy costume emerged from it.

"Have you seen a large sheep dog around here?" the young man queried.

"Can't say I have, pardner," he drawled.

Bert, meanwhile, had circled the sound stage they had been working in and ran as far as the parking lot near the studio entrance. The only animal he saw was a lion on a leash, yawning lazily near a van marked THE LION FARM. His trainer was coaxing him to climb into the truck.

"No luck," the Bobbsey boys told Mr. Kordel when they returned to the stage.

"Then we'll move to the back lot for the garage scene. Waldo's not in that. It'll take the crew a while to set their cameras up there. So why don't you run lines now?"

"Run lines?" Flossie asked. "Like this?"

She jogged in place, dimpling her face in a big grin.

"Study your part, dear," the man said and tweaked her nose.

"Oh," Freddie said, suddenly understanding.

"You can use one of the portable dressing rooms outside. Nobody will bother you in there. Ask one of the crew to drive you to the back lot when you're ready to go."

As soon as the twins stepped into the trailer unit, which contained a built-in bench, dressing table, mirror, closet, and toilet, Freddie noticed a newspaper folded on the table. The front-page story was about a big bank robbery in San Diego, California.

"Let's catch those robbers!" the little boy exclaimed gleefully.

"We don't have time to talk about real mysteries now," Nan said.

Freddie pulled out the small key he had discovered on Waldo. "We can't even talk about this?" he asked, puckering his brow.

"No, Freddie. We have to learn our lines, fast."

The young detective pouted and put the key back in his pocket.

"Okay," Nan said, opening the script to one of the later scenes. "This takes place at an old weather-beaten garage, where we discover a jeep with New Jersey license plates."

"The jeep belongs to the crook who stole the gold coins from a museum," Bert added. "Of

course, at this point in the story we are not supposed to know that. But since we saw it parked
near the cave tunnel where we found one of the
coins—"

"And saw the thief," Nan put in.

"We figure the jeep and the crook go together," Freddie said.

The children took a moment to read through
the scene and memorize it.

"Are you ready?" Nan asked.

The others said yes.

"Peter, someone's coming!" She said her first
line of dialogue.

"Quick, hide, Cindy! You two come with me!"

"I'm s-scared, Pete!" was Flossie's line.

"Don't be. You and Adam stick close to me. I
want to get a close look at the guy who drives this
heap."

The children were so intent on their scripts
that they did not notice the purring of an engine.
When the trailer started to move, they jumped.

"Hey, stop!" Bert called out the door.

But the driver did not hear him. He pulled
ahead toward the back lot at a high speed.

"Maybe he's going to take us to the garage,"
Nan said.

Through the window of the door, she watched
the shells of buildings—offices and fronts of
houses that had often appeared in their favorite
TV shows—whip past them.

"There's Wayne Little!" Nan exclaimed. "And there's the garage!"

"But we're not stopping," Bert said.

He glimpsed through the window in time to see the back end of the garage, where cameras were being set up.

"Where are we going?" Flossie asked.

"I don't know, but we can't go far," Bert replied.

"I don't know about that," Nan said. "I read that this studio has more than five hundred buildings, and acres and acres of woods and fields."

"Terrific." Her twin brother frowned.

As the trailer left the buildings behind, it sped up. Soon it climbed a steep hill to a rocky cliff overlooking a grassy terrain.

"Brace yourselves," Nan said, stretching her arms out in front of the younger twins seated beside her on the bench.

The trailer halted suddenly, then began to back up. Its rear wheels slipped over the edge of the precipice. Loosened stones crumbled beneath. The wheels sank deeper.

"Stop!" Bert shouted, beating his fists against the wall.

CHAPTER III

DRESSING-ROOM MISHAP

"PLEASE stop!" Nan cried loudly.

Freddie and Flossie remained silent while Bert shoved the door of the trailer open.

"I'm going to jump," he declared.

"Don't!" Nan begged.

"You'll get hurt real bad," said Freddie.

His twin sister whimpered. "Please don't, Bert," she said.

"See that tree?" Bert said to his brother. "We're going to aim for that big branch, then fall. You get on my back and hold on as tight as you can."

The wheels of the trailer spun through broken stones, sending a cloud of dust over the boys.

"I'm afraid," Freddie admitted, coughing.

"Quit talking and move!" Bert urged and bent down to let the small boy anchor himself.

The girls gulped as they gazed at the thick limb of the tree, whose roots were as twisted as its trunk. "We'll follow you," Nan said.

"Ready?" Bert asked Freddie.

"Mm-hmm."

The little boy's reply was punctuated by a loud pop! One of the trailer's rear wheels flattened against a rock. The van threatened to overturn.

Bert took a deep breath, swung his arms forward, and jumped toward the tree. His fingers grazed the edge of a smaller branch, cracking it.

"Break!" he told Freddie.

In a split second, the two had barely cleared the gnarled roots protruding through the rocky soil. They fell side by side on the grassy slope and tumbled a short distance. Nan and Flossie, on the other hand, had caught the thick branch.

"All set, Floss?" Nan said, as she surveyed the ground below.

"I can't hold on anymore."

"I'm going to swing out as much as I can. When I say 'go,' you let go, okay?"

"Okay."

Flossie's weight on Nan's back made it difficult for the older sister to move. She gritted her teeth and tensed her arms. Her hands, wet with perspiration, slipped on the bark. She pulled her body back as far as she could and swung forward.

"Go!" Nan cried.

Flossie broke away and somersaulted onto the grass. Nan rolled clear of her sister. Both girls stopped within inches of their brothers.

"Are you in one piece?" the boys asked.

"Uh-huh. How about you?"

"Hey, look up there!" Freddie suddenly exclaimed.

"The back end of the trailer is breaking off," Nan observed.

"And it's going to rip right into us," Bert said. "Let's get out of here—"

There was a loud squeal of metal rubbing against metal as the dressing-room snapped away from the front cab. It pitched back and spun down the hill toward the children. Quickly they ran out of its path, stumbling through tall clumps of weed and uncut grass. Before the Bobbseys could speak, the dressing room had crashed into a tree and tipped over.

"Whew!" Bert sighed. "That was a close one!"

"Too close for me." Nan gasped.

Flossie threw her chubby arms around her sister's waist and wept.

"Don't cry," Freddie said. "Nobody got hurt."

"I know," Flossie sniffled, "but we could have been." Big tears rolled down her face.

The older twins caught sight of a man emerging from the front of the trailer. "Stay back," said Bert. He pulled everyone behind some low bushes. "I want to see what he does."

The trailer spun down the hill toward the Bobbseys!

"Can you see him, Bert?" Nan asked, squinting in the strong sunlight.

"Not too well."

"Do you think he knew we were in the dressing room?" Freddie asked.

"I don't know," said his brother. "But if he did—"

"Then he must've been trying to get rid of us," Nan commented.

"Oh, I don't think he really wanted to harm us," Bert said. "The tire blew out and that threw the trailer off balance."

"So, if he wasn't trying to hurt us," Nan went on, "what was he doing?"

"Maybe he was hoping he could keep us out of that garage scene."

"But why?"

Bert did not reply. He kept his eyes glued on the mysterious figure who stared across the grassy slope at the overturned dressing room.

"It looks like he can't make up his mind whether to climb down here or not," noted Bert. "Guess it's too steep for him."

As Bert said this, the man stepped back into the cab and pulled away.

"He'll probably drive down to see how much damage was done," Nan said.

"Maybe. Maybe not," her twin replied. He glanced at his watch, which fortunately had not broken in the fall. "It's almost four o'clock. Kord is really going to think we jinxed his show."

"Will he fire us?" Freddie asked.

"I hope not."

"It wasn't our fault," put in Flossie.

"Shh," Bert suddenly interrupted. "Listen!"

The sound of an approaching vehicle grew louder.

"That's him!" Nan exclaimed in a whisper.

"Shh," her brother cautioned her. "Keep it down, everybody."

The truck came into view, apparently heading toward the overturned dressing room, but instead cutting past it into a thickly wooded area. When the vehicle was out of sight, the four young detectives emerged from their hiding place. Freddie was the first to examine the dressing room.

"Boy, it's all messed up," he said. "Broken mirror."

"Watch out for glass," his older sister warned. She moved carefully around the unit.

"It's badly bent," Bert observed. "It'll have to be towed away."

"Come on," urged Flossie. "We'd better see Mr. Kordel."

The tired children started to walk back.

"Mr. Haberman is going to have put fresh make-up on us," Freddie said, looking at his twin's smudged face. "You've got lipstick on your forehead, Floss. How'd it get way up there?"

"I don't know."

"We're lucky we don't have any broken

bones," Nan said. "Bert, how are we going to explain all of this to Kord, especially when he sees the mud and grass stains on our clothes?"

"I'm not sure, but I think we ought to wait until after we shoot our scene before we say anything."

"But he's going to ask us!" Freddie piped up.

"Of course he is, but—" Bert paused. "I hear something. Do you?"

Everyone stopped walking. An engine rumbled in the distance.

"Maybe it's the same guy again," Nan said.

"I doubt it," her twin replied.

Shortly, a large white truck with the name Globe Television Studios stamped on its side pulled out from behind a mountain of bushes. Flossie darted after it.

"Stop! Stop!" she shouted.

Bert whistled while Nan and Freddie clapped their hands and waved. The truck halted and a man in a cowboy costume opened the rear door. He recognized Freddie and smiled.

"Didn't I see you at Stage Twenty-four?" he asked.

"Yes," the little boy answered. "Can we get a ride to a garage?"

"On the back lot," Bert quickly added.

"Sure thing. Hop on. We're heading in that direction."

"Thanks," Nan said. "We really appreciate it."

The children climbed quickly into the back of the truck. A couple of men, wearing Indian head-dresses made of blue beads and feathers, and pants that looked like animal skins, sat on crates.

"Come here, sweetie," one man said to Flossie. "You sit on this box."

"Are you a real Indian?" she asked him.

"No, I'm an actor. I'm making a movie."

"About cowboys and Indians?"

"Sort of," he said. "But it's not an old-time cowboy and Indian movie. Indians were always put down in those films. They never won any battles against the white man, that's for sure.

"We're doing a take-off on the Old West pictures. It's really funny. It's about a guy who gets lost in the hills of Texas and finds himself in the middle of an Indian reservation. He has some outdated ideas about what Indians are like and we decide to play some tricks on him," the man said. "But enough about me. What are you kids doing here at Globe Studios?"

"We are in the first TV show in a new series called *The Young Detectives*. It will be on in September."

"Are you going to be in all of the stories?"

"There are supposed to be different kids starring from week to week. We may do a few guest spots, though," Bert replied. "But it would be hard for us to be in all the shows. We live in Lakeport and we have lots of stuff to do there."

"That's right," added Freddie. "We solve mysteries and go to school."

"Oh, I see."

When the truck reached the garage, Marcy and the director were talking. They looked worried.

"Hi!" the twins called out as they scrambled off the truck.

"What happened to you?" Marcy gasped, studying their smudged faces and clothes.

"Where have you been?" Mr. Kordel snapped. "Don't tell me now. We've got plenty to do."

"But—" Marcy began. "These children—"

"No buts about it," the director said. "I've lost too much sunlight already. And this scene needs every bit of it."

The young woman took the children aside briefly. "Are you all right?"

"We're fine," Nan assured her. "Really we are. We'll tell you all about it later."

"Then you'd better change quickly. You can't appear in those clothes."

The children were escorted to a dressing room set up at the entrance to the garage. Marcy followed them.

"Here," she said, handing the girls an envelope. "It's a mailgram addressed to all of you, in care of the studio."

"Maybe it's a fan letter!" Nan said, excited.

She opened it and read quietly.

"What does it say. What does it say?" Flossie insisted.

The older girl cleared her throat. "It says, 'Tried to reach you by phone this morning. Emergency. Come home immediately. Dad.'"

CHAPTER IV

MAILGRAM MYSTERY

NAN read the message again. "We should call home right away, Floss."

"Let's tell Freddie and Bert."

Before Marcy could stop her, the little girl had scooted next door and knocked.

"Who is it?" came the older boy's voice.

"It's me. Flossie."

"What's up?"

"Daddy wants us to go home."

"Huh?" Bert replied, opening the door.

Nan peered around hers. "That's right."

"I'll phone for you while you get dressed for your scene," Marcy offered. "Okay?"

The young detectives hesitated but agreed at last.

"Will you tell Dad that we'll contact him as soon as we have a chance?" Bert said.

"Sure, sure."

Without saying another word, Marcy dashed out of the dressing room toward John Kordel. She told him about the message from Mr. Bobbsey.

"We've already filmed five pages of script," he declared. "It's too late to replace these children. We've got a very tight production schedule, but if they have to go home—"

"There's nothing you can do," Marcy finished his sentence. "Can someone drive me to the front lot to make my long-distance call?"

"Wayne, will you send a car over here for Marcy?" the director said to his assistant.

Meanwhile, the twins had put on fresh clothes. Abe Haberman had checked their make-up, and the hairstylist had combed their hair.

"Do you remember your lines?" Nan asked Flossie as they headed for the garage.

"I think so."

"Do you?" Bert asked his twin.

"I hope so. I've got Mother and Dad on the brain, though."

"Me too," said Freddie.

The Bobbseys did not discuss the worrisome mailgram. They plunged into their scene. John Kordel walked them into the garage where an old jeep stood. He gazed out at the two large square frames of silvery foil atop high metal tripods. The foil caught the sunlight and bounced it into the garage.

"Don't look at those reflectors if you can help it," the director said. "They'll blind you."

The children nodded.

"Now here's the scene," he went on. "You have just discovered the jeep. You hear somebody coming and you decide to hide. I know the script tells you at that point to run out of the garage and hide behind its door. I'd like to add something. Before you exit, duck down behind the car. Then, when you think you're in the clear, run like mad. Got that?"

"I think so," Bert said.

The twins went through the scene easily.

"Cut," the director said when they finished it. "That was fine. Now I want to do the scene at the garage just before this one."

"Where we are looking for footprints," Nan said.

"One and the same."

"We have just arrived at the garage, right?" Freddie asked.

"Yes."

"The garage doors are closed. You look for footprints. They match the ones you saw near the cave. You open the garage and surprise!" Mr. Kordel beamed.

"It's the jeep with the New Jersey license plates!" Flossie exclaimed.

The cameras, lights, and sun reflectors were

moved back on the gravel driveway leading to the garage.

"How's your nose?" the make-up man asked Flossie as he brushed some powder on it.

He checked the other Bobbseys while the hairstylist ran a comb through their hair again. Then, once more, they stood before the cameras. Bert was in the lead.

"Follow me!" he whispered.

"Peter?"

"What is it, Cindy?"

"That crook could be watching us."

"Fat chance of that."

"Sure he could," piped up one of the smaller children.

"Stick close."

Dialogue stopped while the young actors crept toward the garage. Upon reaching it, though, it was Nan's turn to speak.

"Look at these footprints," she said, kneeling to examine them closely. "The star in the center of the left sole is exactly like the one we saw near the cave."

"These are fresh prints, too," her twin brother said.

"Here are some more," the younger children said. They stood by the doors to the garage.

Cautiously, the older detectives pulled open the door. They gasped at the sight of the jeep.

"It's the same car. Should we look in it?" the younger girl said.

"Look at these footprints!" the girl detective said.

"Maybe he put the gold coins in the trunk," said her twin.

"Cut," the director said. "That's great. We can close shop for the night."

Marcy, who had watched part of the final scene, sparkled. "You were fantastic!"

"Thanks, Marcy," Nan said. "Did you talk to my father?"

"I certainly did. There's no emergency at home."

"There isn't?"

"No, everything is fine and dandy in Lakeport."

"So Dad didn't send us that mailgram?" Bert asked.

"Guess not."

"That's strange," Flossie said.

"Very," commented Freddie.

"Do you have any hunches about who would mail you such a thing?" Marcy inquired, as John Kordel joined them.

"What's up?" he interrupted.

The children told him what Marcy had found out.

"That's wonderful news!" he said, delighted. "You're the only ones I want in this show. I would have been unhappy about looking for replacements."

Flossie tugged on his arm. "Somebody doesn't want us around here. They want us to leave California."

"Maybe it's the same guy who tried to strand us out on the cliff," Bert said, then stopped himself.

The director had forgotten about the earlier delay of the afternoon. The question suddenly struck him again.

"Please tell us where you were and why you were so late for this last scene?" he asked the children.

"Well—" Nan began.

"Well—" Bert stumbled, then he recounted what had happened to them in the portable dressing room.

"How awful!" Marcy exclaimed. "And you're not hurt?"

The twins shook their heads.

"You must have the studio doctor look at you."

"May we do something else first?" the older boy requested. "I'd like to show you where the accident occurred."

"Yes," Nan agreed, "before the sun goes down."

The director accompanied the Bobbseys and Marcy to the back lot in the small station wagon that was used to run errands for the film crew. When they arrived in the vicinity of the cliff, the twins were stunned.

"It's gone!" Freddie cried.

"The dressing room's gone!" Flossie joined in.

The young detectives rushed from the car to the familiar tree the trailer had hit. There were a few chips of mirror and paint on the ground.

"Where did it go?" the little girl asked, confused.

"Maybe the man did come back for it after all," Nan suggested.

"Probably," Bert said. He stared at the heavy brush underfoot. It had been pressed down in two even rows. "Those are wheel marks."

"This sounds like a familiar scene," the director commented to Marcy. "We could put it in their TV show."

The Bobbseys followed the marks a short distance, then stopped.

"The grass is too heavy. I can't tell where those wheels went."

"Let's go back," said Marcy. "You've had a long day, and you have another long one ahead of you tomorrow."

After a stop at studio security to report the dressing-room mishap, the children were examined by the doctor on duty. As they had insisted, they had suffered no injuries during their fall.

"We'd better call Mother and Dad." Nan yawned as they reached their hotel. "Bert, why don't you and Freddie come to our room. We'll phone from there."

When Nan opened the door, she froze. All of her clothes and Flossie's were strewn across the floor. Bureau drawers had been pulled out and overturned. Pages from her extra copy of the television script lay torn in shreds!

"Oh, no!" Nan quivered.

"Wha—" Marcy gulped.

Without wasting a second, Bert and Freddie dashed to their room, which adjoined the girls and Marcy's suite, then ran back.

"The same tornado hit our room!" Bert cried.

CHAPTER V

FILM CLUE

"Has anything been stolen?" Marcy asked the twins.

Nan and Flossie scanned the clothing on the floor. The younger girl began to pick up a blouse.

"Floss, you'd better leave everything where it is," Nan said. "We ought to report this to the hotel manager."

"And the police," added Bert.

While his twin sister dialed the reception desk, Bert went to his room to call the police. In less than a half hour, the hotel manager and two policemen were gaping at the ransacked rooms.

"Did you have anything of special value with you?" one officer questioned the Bobbseys.

"No, sir," Freddie replied.

"Do you have any idea why anyone might have done this?" the other man inquired.

"No, sir," Flossie said. " 'Cept we think somebody's been trying to keep us from doing a TV show."

"Oh?"

The little girl told him what had happened to the children earlier that day. Marcy explained that Globe Studios had asked her to chaperone the Bobbseys and that she would keep close watch on them from now on.

"Perhaps you would prefer to switch to another location in the hotel," the manager suggested after the police left.

"That's a good idea," Nan said.

As quickly as they could, the twins packed their things and were sent to a suite of rooms on the top floor.

"Wow!" Bert exclaimed as he opened his door.

Ahead of him was a floor-to-ceiling window that spanned one wall. Lights of buildings twinkled in the distance against the dark sky. When the twins were settled in their respective rooms, Marcy called them together.

"Maybe you can help *me* solve a mystery!" she said.

"What kind of mystery?" Flossie replied.

"We thought the only mysteries we'd find at the TV studio would be the storybook kind!" Nan chuckled.

"Just a moment," Marcy excused herself.

She returned with a roll of film in one hand and a camera in the other. "I found this film near the studio's visitor center. It was on the grass. I checked at the center to see if anybody had reported that it was missing. Nobody had," Marcy said. "I also found this." She indicated the camera.

"With the film?" Bert asked.

"As a matter of fact, no. I noticed it on a bench outside the studio entrance. As you can see the strap is unbuckled. It probably slipped off somebody's shoulder while he was sitting. Anyway, it's a valuable camera, and I think we ought to try to find the owner."

"Is there any film in it?" Nan asked. "If so, it could be a clue to the owner's identity."

Her twin brother tapped a finger to his forehead. "Smart thinking," he complimented her.

"When did you find all of this, Marcy?" Nan questioned.

"Yesterday," she said. "I would have shown it to you before now, but there was so much going on at the studio. You had scripts to learn. I just forgot about it."

"Did you look through the lost-and-found columns of the newspaper?" Nan went on.

"Yes. There were no ads for cameras."

Meanwhile, Bert examined the camera. Several pictures had already been taken.

"We ought to use the remaining film so we

can develop it along with the other roll," Marcy said.

As she snapped pictures of the Bobbseys, Freddie spoke. "Marcy, could you do us a favor?"

"Sure," she said, clicking the camera.

"Would you drive us to see Mr. Willis?"

"Waldo's trainer?"

"Hm-mm."

"First thing in the morning, after you've called your parents and had a good night's sleep."

"What time do we have to be on the set tomorrow?" Nan inquired.

"It's on the call sheet," Marcy answered.

Flossie rolled back the bedspread of her bed, then the blanket. "I don't see anything on the sheet."

"Not that sheet," Bert said. "Marcy means the long piece of paper we all get that tells you what time everybody in the crew and cast has to be ready to work."

Nan dug through her suitcase and found the wrinkled paper. "Bert and Freddie have to be in make-up at noon. Flossie and I have to be there by twelve-thirty," she said. "Do you know where Mr. Willis lives?"

"In the valley," Marcy replied, "so we'd better allow plenty of travel time to go and come back."

The twins agreed that they would go to bed early.

"Right after supper we will," Freddie said.

"Right after we call home," Nan put in.

"And after we unpack," Bert added.

"We have to go over our lines before tomorrow too," Flossie declared.

Marcy sighed and smiled. "You're real troopers!"

Just before they were ready to say good night, they glanced at their scripts. Freddie got down on all fours.

"Who are you s'posed to be?" his twin sister asked.

"Who do you think? The Six-Million-Dollar Kid?" he giggled and sidled up to Nan.

She petted his curly hair. "Good boy, Waldo," she said, starting off the scene that was to be filmed the next day. "We have to be real quiet. The thieves are in that cabin over there."

"Waldo" sniffed the rug and sneezed.

"Waldo's not s'posed to sneeze!" Flossie declared.

"You blew your line, Freddie!" his brother teased. "Bark, dog, bark!"

The young detectives laughed and yawned. They put away their scripts shortly. That night they all fell into deep sleep. Flossie dreamed of herself and Freddie riding a pony.

"After him, Freddie!" she cried.

Waldo was running ahead of them. His shaggy ears flapped in the wind beneath the band of feathers that circled his head. A pack of arrows was strapped to his back.

"After him, Freddie!" Flossie cried.

"Don't go away, Waldo!" Flossie begged. "Stop, Waldo. Please stop!"

But the animal did not stop. It raced wildly across a grassy field and led the riders up and down a steep hill into a desert. There a young woman with full dark hair held a giant camera. She flashed picture after picture of the trio heading toward her. Large balls of light danced in front of the children's eyes. Flossie blinked. Morning sun was streaming across her face.

At breakfast, Marcy greeted the twins with a big hug. "First we'll drop off the film, then we'll drive out to see Slim. How does that sound?"

"Great," Nan said.

They found a camera shop that offered to develop the rolls of film within a few hours. By nine o'clock the group was riding on the coastal highway that stretched along the Pacific Ocean and its wide beaches.

"What are those big black things going up and down in the water?" Flossie asked.

"Oil rigs. They're pumping for oil under the sea," Marcy explained.

She turned off the main road onto a narrow one that led inland to a small town, its streets lined with a few shops that had shell jewelry hanging in front of their windows.

"There aren't many houses around here, are there?" said Marcy. "Or at least, they aren't built close to each other."

"There's a sign for Willis," Bert remarked.

Marcy pulled up in front of the modest, stucco house. It was set back from the road.

"Somebody ought to cut the grass," Bert commented as the children stepped out of the car.

"Do you want to volunteer?" Nan asked.

"Not me," he said, feeling the grass crunch underfoot. "But I hope Willis takes better care of his animals."

"My husband's not home!" a woman at the front door suddenly called out to the visitors.

"How does she know you want to see her husband?" Marcy said.

"Good question," Nan replied. "Slim must be inside. Saw us coming—"

"And told his wife to tell us he's not in!" Bert continued.

"You kids have seen too many movies!" Marcy chuckled.

"May we talk to you a minute?" Bert asked the woman politely.

She hesitated, then stepped back as a hand yanked the front door open. Slim Willis stood before them.

"What do you want?" he asked.

"We want to talk to you about Waldo?" Freddie spoke.

"What about Waldo?"

"May we show you something?" Freddie went on.

"Oh, I suppose so," the man said, obviously irritated.

Mrs. Willis, a petite woman with short red hair and icy blue eyes, followed the twins and Marcy inside.

"Have a seat," she said, indicating an overstuffed couch.

"Well, what is it?" her husband asked the children. "I don't have time to waste. I've got things to do out back in my coop."

"Do you have chickens?" Freddie inquired.

"Never mind, little boy. Now show me what you've got."

Freddie pulled the small key from his pocket. "I found this on Waldo," he said.

"Maybe it will help us find him," Flossie said.

"Hmm," the man responded. "Sam, come meet the Bobbseys!"

As if from nowhere, a large white bird soared into the living room toward Freddie!

CHAPTER VI

PUZZLING PESTER

"Oops!" Freddie exclaimed as the big white bird swooped toward him.

He lifted one arm to his head and ducked. The other Bobbseys gasped as the bird perched on their brother's wrist.

"He won't hurt you," the trainer said.

"You're a friendly guy, aren't you, Sam?" Mrs. Willis remarked. "Sam's a cockatoo."

The bird squawked and snatched the key out of Freddie's hand.

"You said you found that on my dog?" Slim asked.

"That's right," Bert replied. "Actually, Freddie was playing with Waldo and he pulled it out in a clump of his hair."

"Oh, I see," the man said. "Sam, bring it to me."

The bird ruffled the white comb of feathers on its head and flew to Mr. Willis.

"Thank you, Sam," the trainer said, taking the key from the bird's beak.

He twirled it between his fingers and handed it to his wife. "Do you know anything about this, dear?"

"Can't say that I do."

"Well, how do you suppose the key got caught in Waldo's hair?" Freddie asked.

"You know that dog's hair mats easily. Maybe he was rolling around on a floor where the key had been dropped," Slim said.

"That's it, Slim," his wife added.

"But Freddie told us the key was stuck near the dog's skin," Bert went on.

"We're not detectives," the woman replied. "We are plain, simple people. We train Waldo but we certainly don't keep track of every little move he makes. If we did, we'd know where he went."

"I'm sorry, kids," Mr. Willis said in a soft voice. "We just don't know anything about this key."

Marcy, who had been quiet during the discussion, now spoke. "Perhaps your agent might be of some help to the Bobbseys," she said. "Would you—"

"Sam," the man interrupted, flicking his wrist slightly. "Please return this."

At the signal, the bird took the key and lifted. It spinned in a circle, turned upside down, then flitted from Bert to Nan to Flossie and finally to Freddie. The key dropped into his lap.

"Thank you, Sam," the boy said.

"As I started to say, Slim," Marcy went on, "maybe your agent—"

"I doubt very much that Pester Davis could tell you anything more."

"What does Mr. Davis do as your agent?" Nan inquired.

"Not much." Mrs. Willis chuckled, then caught her husband's frown.

"Pester makes all my deals for me. When a studio needs certain animals for shows, they call him. He finds out what tricks the animals need to know and tells me. I get a copy of the script and go right to work."

"How'd he get the name Pester?" Bert asked.

"He pesters people until they make a deal with him," Marcy replied.

"Do you know him?" Flossie whispered in her ear.

"Yes, I do. He has gotten jobs for some of my friends."

"Well, thank you, Mr. and Mrs. Willis." Bert ended the discussion.

"Just call me Slim."

"Please return this key, Sam." Slim said.

"And I'm Edith."

On the way back, the twins asked Marcy if they had time to stop by the talent agent's office.

"Plenty," she said, swinging the car toward Beverly Hills. "I'll drop you off in front and park the car."

Soon they pulled in front of a tall bank building opposite the famous Beverly Wilshire Hotel.

"Here we are," Marcy declared.

"We'll wait for you in the lobby," Bert said and shut the car door.

"I wonder who that is," Flossie said.

A long, black limousine had just driven under the red canopy at the hotel entrance. The doorman, in a gold-trimmed suit, tall black hat, and white gloves, was opening the limousine door. A handsome young man with dark hair and almond-shaped eyes emerged as Marcy rejoined the children.

"Is he an actor?" Freddie asked, excited.

"No, I don't think so," their chaperone said. "But he looks very familiar."

"Can we get his autograph?" Bert and Nan interjected.

Before Marcy could reply, the twins had darted across the street. Bert held out a small pencil and piece of paper to the man, who smiled.

"What are your names?" he asked the four-some. "Aren't you in a new television series?" he added, when he heard the name Bobbsey.

The twins nodded as he wrote "Best Wishes on your new TV show. Dino Anagnost" and handed the message to Flossie.

"Thank you, Mr. Angus-sauce."

Bert nudged his small sister and repeated the name properly. When they returned to Marcy, they showed her the man's distinctive signature.

"He's a very well-known conductor."

"On a train?" Flossie asked, wrinkling her face.

"No, honey, of orchestras and choirs," Marcy said, as the group went through the revolving doors to an elevator.

"He's the first famous person we've met here so far," Freddie commented.

"If you stayed around Beverly Hills all day, you'd see several," Marcy said. "Lots of important people live in this community—artists, musicians, executives of movie studios and television networks."

The elevator stopped and opened onto a wood-paneled hallway with soft lights shining on the names of office doors. The one for Pester Davis was ajar. A woman wearing rhinestone-framed glasses slid them down her nose as the Bobbsey twins entered.

"May I help you?" she asked.

"We would like to see Mr. Davis," Nan said.

"Do you have an appointment?"

"No, but—"

Well, then I'm afraid it's out of the question. Mr. Davis is a very busy man today."

As she spoke, a door behind her opened revealing a curly-haired young man. "Talk to you tomorrow," he said to the man inside.

"Hi, Glen!" Marcy exclaimed.

"Marcy! I haven't seen you since we did that box-office smash *Oodles of Poodles*."

"I never heard of it," Nan admitted.

"Nobody else has either." Marcy laughed. "The studio hasn't released it yet to the movie theaters. It's a comedy. Glen and I had small parts in it—my first acting role since I moved to California. Acting is what I love to do most, but I haven't had much of a chance to do it. I've been so busy—"

"Doing public relatives!" Flossie giggled.

"And looking after us," Nan added.

"Can I have your autograph?" Freddie asked Glen.

"Be glad to."

He whipped off a signature on a piece of paper and handed it to the little girl.

"See you, Marcy," he said to her.

"Now go right in," she told the twins, indicating the still-open door to Mr. Davis's office.

"You can't go in there!" the receptionist huffed.

"These are the Bobbsey twins, who are—"

"Oh," Mr. Davis interrupted. "You were signed to play the leads in the first show of the new TV series. Come in."

"We're looking for Waldo sheep dog," Flossie began the conversation.

"I don't understand."

"Didn't anybody notify you that Waldo disappeared from the sound stage we were working on?" Bert asked.

The man shook his head in bafflement. "I still don't understand what that has to do with me."

"Don't you work with Slim Willis?" Nan asked.

"Yes. Oh, oh, oh you're talking about Willis's dog Waldo. I didn't know he was lost." He buzzed the receptionist. "Carey, have Arlene Sidaris and Joyce Brotman arrived yet?"

"They're waiting to see you," the voice said.

"Please forgive me for rushing you out so quickly. But I have a rather urgent meeting now. I just can't spare the time to talk to you now."

"But—" Nan said.

Mr. Davis swung out of his chair and walked toward the door. "I am terribly sorry."

"Could we see you tomorrow?" Bert asked.

"I'm afraid not. I have to fly out of town."

"What about the next day?"

"No, I am really tied up this week."

Disappointed, the children left the office. "We're getting nowhere fast," said Bert.

"Right," Marcy said, glancing at her watch, "we

had better head for the studio right away. It's after eleven."

"We have to be in make-up in another hour," Bert said.

Once they were out of the busy shopping area, Marcy drove toward a canyon road that cut through the mountain to Globe City. It slowly narrowed into two lanes that curved high into the hills. On each side, ranch-style houses with bay windows that looked across valleys jutted out on small cliffs covered with palm trees.

"They're bee-yoo-ti-ful!" Flossie exclaimed.

Marcy's eyes, however, were glued to the road. She noticed a man on a motorcycle behind her. His face was hidden by a helmet. He shot forward, keeping close to her car.

"I'd like to get rid of that tailgater," she said and pressed her foot on the gas pedal.

Again the motorcyclist sped after her.

"It's dangerous to play tag on a canyon road," Marcy went on, gripping the steering wheel tightly.

Bert and Freddie waved the man back, but he would not pay attention. He rolled his motorcycle close to the bumper of the car and touched it.

"Is he trying to force us off the road?" Nan asked nervously.

She gazed ahead at a break in the hill where the road swung over a ravine.

"Be careful, Marcy," Nan said.

Suddenly the motorcyclist darted past the twins' car and weaved in front of it. He cut his speed, causing Marcy to lift her foot from the pedal.

"We'll never get to the studio in time." Freddie panicked.

"Yes, you will," Marcy said, biting her lips.

Confident that no car was coming toward her from the opposite lane, she pulled out to pass the motorcyclist and whizzed ahead.

"Watch out!" the twins shrieked. In the path of the fast-moving vehicles was a blur of white and gray.

"It's Waldo!" Flossie screeched.

CHAPTER VII

"MONSTER" TWINS

FLOSSIE and Freddie shut their eyes as Marcy swerved the car back into the right lane.

"Don't hit Waldo!" the little girl cried. She sank against her seat.

The shaggy dog leaped off the road into a cluster of large plants while the motorcyclist swung his bike to the left. He jumped over a low hedge, cycled on grass a short distance, then returned to the road and zipped away.

"Where's Waldo?" Freddie asked.

"He's gone. He's gone," said his twin, who peered through the back window.

"We'll find him," Marcy said.

"Don't worry, Floss," Nan comforted her sister.

"At least we got rid of that crazy guy on the

motorcycle," Bert declared. "You're a terrific driver, Marcy."

She slowed the car to a stop. The boys jumped out and ran back several yards.

"Do you see him?" the older one asked his brother.

"Nope."

They pushed between the plants Waldo had trampled. Beyond them were others whose tall, stiff leaves and orange, bird-shaped flowers lay in a broken trail.

"Come on," Bert said.

"Waldo's gone forever!" Freddie said, following close to Bert.

"He just got scared by the car," the boy replied. "Waldo!" he called out.

"Waldo!" Freddie chimed in.

There was no response, only the drone of a low-flying plane. The pair trekked past the plants into broad patches of weed. They discovered a few clumps of the dog's shaggy hair but no paw prints.

"Let's give up," Bert said.

Dejected, they turned back. Marcy and the girls did not have to ask what Bert and Freddie had discovered.

"Zero," said the older boy as they stepped into the car.

En route to the studio, the twins discussed the motorcyclist. "He rode that motorcycle like Evil Knievel," Bert commented.

"Maybe he was Evil Knievel," Freddie said.

"Or somebody like him—maybe a stuntman."

"Why was he doing all of those stunts?" Nan wondered.

Marcy glanced at her watch. "I don't know, but Kord is going to have a fit if I don't get you all to make-up on time today."

She sped toward the studio and let the boys out at the stage where the cave-tunnel scene had been filmed earlier.

"We'd like to check with security, Marcy, about the dressing room that overturned in the back lot," Nan said.

"While you go there, I'll see if any of the pictures have been developed yet. I'll meet you on-stage."

The group split in different directions. Bert and Freddie were being seated in front of tables with boxes of tissue and make-up on them.

"So, you're supposed to be in disguise for this scene," Abe said to the boys.

"Tony, you work on Freddie while I do Bert," he addressed his assistant.

"Do you mind if we go over our lines a little?" the older Bobbsey asked.

"Not a bit," the men replied.

"Freddie," Bert began, "this is the scene at the cave tunnel, where we are searching for the gold coins, right?"

"Uh-huh. We just found a couple of coins at

the top of the path leading down to the tunnel."

"So my first line is, 'I'm glad we decided to wear disguises this time,' " Bert said.

"Me too, 'specially something that will camouflage us in this cave.' "

"Excuse me, son," Abe interrupted. "I'm afraid you're going to have to close your mouth while I put on this brown cream."

"Better close your eyes too," his assistant added.

After a minute, Bert asked, "Can I talk now?"

"Go ahead."

"Hey," the boy went on with his script, "what happened to that arrow Cindy and I found?"

"Maybe it washed off."

"Couldn't have. It was too high on the wall for the water to reach it. I think somebody removed it."

"Excuse me again," Abe said, patting powder on the boy's cheekbones. "Now I'll put on a liquid base."

"And then," the other make-up man added, "we'll highlight your chins with these brushes."

Layer upon layer of make-up was applied to the brothers' faces.

"Bert, I forget my next line," Freddie said.

"Look at your script later," the older boy mumbled between his heavily powdered lips.

"Voilà!" exclaimed the two men. "You're done!"

The Bobbseys sat forward and stared in amazement at each other.

"Is that me?" They blinked in the mirror.

"Is that you?" Bert asked Freddie, laughing loudly.

"We look like monster twins!" the small boy bubbled.

"Fabulous, Abe. Fabulous, Tony," the director congratulated the make-up men upon seeing the young detectives.

Flossie squirmed when Freddie darted toward her. "Ooh, yicky!" she said, touching a greenish brown wrinkle across her twin's forehead.

"It's our turn, Floss," Nan said. "Let's go."

"Just a second," came Marcy's familiar voice. "Look at these!"

She removed several photographs from a small yellow envelope. The twins studied them, puzzled.

"Who wants to look at any old bank?" Flossie asked, glancing at one or two pictures.

"A robber, that's who," her sister said.

"Somebody went to a lot of trouble to take different views of one place," Bert observed.

"How do you know all of the pictures are of the same bank?" Nan asked.

"I just figured that was the case."

"Look at this picture and that other one," Nan said. "They seem to be of the same front entrance. But there's a tall tree next to one."

"Look at these pictures!" Marcy exclaimed.

"And nothing next to the other," her twin pointed out. "You win. It's true that at least two of these pictures are not of the same bank."

"You're quite a detective, Nan." Marcy complimented her.

"Marcy, were these pictures in the camera or on the roll of film you found?" Freddie asked.

"Gee, I don't know," she said. "Here's the other set too."

She pulled out a second bulky envelope. In it were a number of pictures of the same baby.

"She's cute," Flossie said.

"And I'd say definitely not related to the first set of pictures," Marcy commented.

"That goes without saying," Bert said.

"Now what do we do?" his twin sister asked.

The other children sighed. "It's too bad we don't know which set of pictures was in the camera," Freddie remarked.

"How much difference would it make?" Bert replied.

"I bet the bank pictures were in the camera," the little boy declared. "We ought to try to find the owner."

"And I bet they weren't," Flossie said.

"Let's take a vote," Marcy insisted.

"That won't help us any," Nan said. "We probably ought to turn the camera and the pictures over to the police."

"Okay, but maybe I ought to have an extra set

made of each in case you want to follow up any clues."

"That's a great idea," Nan said.

While she and her younger sister went to the make-up area, their brothers picked up their scripts again. The floor of the metal pit had been repaired and water was being quickly pumped in.

"Freddie, take a look at that guy!" Bert said suddenly.

He noticed the sleek figure of a man in a leather vest. He was holding a motorcyclist's helmet.

CHAPTER VIII

CATWALK TRAP

"Do you think that's the motorcyclist who was following us on the canyon road?"

"I sure do."

As the boys pulled closer to him, they overheard John Kordel say, "The final decision about who was to be in this show was not mine. You ought to talk to the producers. Maybe they can put your brother and sister in the next episode."

The husky man grumbled and pushed past Bert and Freddie to a side door.

"Mister," the little boy called after him. "We want to talk to you."

The door slammed shut.

"Boy, he was in a big hurry," Bert said to the director.

"Grady's always running somewhere," Kord replied. "He's one of the studio's best stuntmen."

"That explains how he jumped that hedge so smoothly back on the canyon road," Bert commented.

"Oh, you've seen some of Grady's fancy footwork on his motorcycle?" the director asked.

"I'll say." Bert frowned. "We almost hit Waldo because of him."

"Waldo? *Our* Waldo? Where is he?"

"We lost him," Freddie said and told the director what happened.

Before he could finish speaking, Wayne Little interrupted. "We're almost ready for picture!" he yelled. "It's TV time, everybody. Hold it down, folks."

Seeing the boys in their monster make-up, he smiled. "You guys look gorgeous," he teased. "You've got that inside-cave glow!"

The brothers lowered themselves into the watery pit and sloshed in front of the cave entrance. Bright lights flooded it as a camera swung in toward the actors.

"Action," the director said after everyone became silent.

"Are you with me, Adam?" began Bert.

"Yeah," the younger one replied, "and I wish I weren't."

"It was your idea to investigate this tunnel for the umpteenth time."

"You only came down here once with Cindy," retorted the other boy.

"Well, it seems like I've been in this cave a million times," was Bert's line. "Listen a minute. That sounds like a motorboat up ahead. Keep back."

After the noise died away, the boys continued to explore the area.

"Adam, do you still have those gold coins we found?"

"Hm-mm. Want 'em?" The younger one fetched two shiny disks from his shirt pocket. "Here—oops!"

The coins slipped between his fingers and plopped into the water.

"Cut!" Mr. Kordel interrupted. "Jay," he said, addressing the crewman in a wet suit, "please get those coins for Freddie. Son, you and Bert go behind the cave and make your entrance again."

As the boys followed his instructions, Nan and Flossie appeared with a large sheep dog.

"Look who came back—Waldo!" Flossie exclaimed gaily.

Everyone stared in the little girl's direction. "Honey, I hate to disappoint you. But that's not Waldo. That's Cheesecake. He's Waldo's replacement," Mr. Kordel told her.

"But he looks exactly like Waldo," she replied.

"I hope so," the man said. "We always make sure our animal suppliers have doubles on hand."

"Is that why there are two sets of twins in this TV story?" Flossie giggled.

"Oh, Flossie." Nan groaned. "Come on, you and Cheesecake ought to study your lines. Let's go over to the dressing tables."

The dog nuzzled Flossie as Nan led them away from the crew and cameras.

"Okey-dokey, doggy," the younger twin said happily. "You stick with me and don't bark."

She glanced at her script briefly, then closed it. She made believe she was climbing down steps at the beginning of the cave tunnel.

"Don't make so much noise," she whispered her first line to the dog.

Cheesecake panted.

"It's spooky in this old cave, isn't it?"

"No, Floss, that's not the line," Nan interrupted her. She was reading her own copy of the story. "You say, 'This old cave gives me goosebumps.' "

From the corner of her eye, the older girl noticed something moving. She glimpsed one of the long wooden beams that spanned the ceiling. One end had snapped and hung precariously.

"Look out, everybody!" Nan cried, pointing to the beam that swayed over the pit and crew surrounding it.

"Run, Freddie!" Bert ordered, helping his brother out of the water.

"You, too, Bert!"

The beam of wood was cracking slowly away from the wall that supported it.

"Out of the way!" one man shouted.

"Watch it, Steve!" another cried as the wood broke off fully.

It plummeted toward a cameraman. He quickly rolled his camera out of its path, barely escaping the hard blow.

"Oh, Cheesecake!" Flossie quivered, clinging to the dog.

The beam spiraled head-on into two lights, shattering them, then bounced to one side of the pit and stopped. Half the stage was thrown into darkness.

"Nan?" Flossie whimpered.

There was no reply. The little girl turned around. Her sister was gone.

"Nan!" she burst out.

Cheesecake barked at the shadow of a figure climbing a ladder at the end of the building. John Kordel, in the meantime, had run toward Flossie.

"Are you all right, honey?"

"Yes, sir," she gulped. "But I don't know where Nan is."

Again Cheesecake barked. The director shot a glance at the same tall ladder that reached the broad beams overhead. Nan slid her foot onto one of them.

"Come down from there!" the director shouted. "Please don't go any farther! You'll get hurt!"

"I'm okay, really, I am," she insisted.

She had caught sight of a figure in black on the other side of the broken beam. Had he caused it to fall? She held her breath and tried not to look down at the concrete floor beneath her.

"If I slip," Nan thought, "I'll go splat!" She panicked. Beads of perspiration trickled down her face and spine as she crept across the wood. The man she was after faded into total darkness.

"Stop, Nan!" another familiar voice called out. "Just stay put and we'll get you!"

It was Wayne Little. He leaped up the ladder as fast as he could and began to crawl after the girl. She weaved slightly, trying to focus dizzily on her quarry.

"I'm okay, Wayne," she said and took one more step.

"Nan, don't move!"

"O-O-oo!" she screamed as she lost her footing.

"Nannnnn!" Her sister gasped. "Oh, Nan!"

The older girl caught the beam with her hands, gripped it tightly. "Help. Help me!" she cried.

"Hang on!" Wayne exclaimed. "Don't let go! We'll be there as fast as we can!"

He continued to move toward Nan while the crew below swung the large crane into position under her.

"I'm scared, Wayne!" Nan said, feeling her hands get wet and slide across the wood.

Meanwhile, Bert and Freddie had spied the

"O-O-oo!" Nan screamed.

same figure Nan had seen. The stranger had leaped down a ladder near the platform that had protected the boys from the flying beam.

"He's gone!" Freddie whispered to his brother.

"Sh! I don't think so. I didn't hear the door open, and there's no other way out of this building."

The pair crept quietly between crates and storage boxes. In the near distance they heard John Kordel's voice.

"Roll that crane right under her. Careful now," he was saying.

"I wonder what's going on out there," Freddie mumbled.

"There he goes!" Bert said as a crack of light shone through the stage door. "He's getting into a van. Freddie, you go back to the set. I want to see where that guy is heading."

"I want to go with you."

"I'll be okay."

"But what about our scene?" Freddie asked.

"It'll be hours before they're ready for us again. I'll be back long before then."

Ducking low, the young detective hurried outside and quietly turned the latch of the van's rear door. "I hope he doesn't budge before I get in," Bert thought, listening to the drone of the engine.

He pulled back the door and swung himself inside.

CHAPTER IX

TOOTH ATTACK

BERT quickly closed the door of the green van as it pulled away.

"I wonder where we're going," the boy thought, peering about the windowless vehicle.

It rumbled a brief distance, then screeched to a sudden stop. The driver's door opened and shut. Bert held his breath and slid to a dark corner.

"I hope he doesn't have to come back here for anything," Bert said to himself. He waited a few long moments, then released the door a crack and peeked outside. "We're still on the studio lot. That's for sure. There's the manmade lake I saw in a studio magazine."

He jumped out of the truck and glimpsed a

man entering the small boathouse at the water's edge. Bert raced to it. His heart pounding hard, he pressed against the wooden door. It creaked softly and opened halfway. He took slow, quiet steps into the empty room.

"He could be behind the door, waiting for me. Better be careful," the boy thought. He swung the door back until it touched the wall. "Whew! He must've gone downstairs."

Ahead of him was a staircase leading below. Except for sunlight that seeped through its small windows, the building was in total darkness. "This is spookier than the cave," Bert concluded.

He descended the steps into the murky cellar, pausing to listen at each step. There was not a sound.

"I know that guy came in here," Bert assured himself as he reached bottom.

Suddenly a light flashed on and off behind a wall. "Where'd that come from? And how do I get back there?"

He followed the length of the wall. There was no door. "That's strange," he thought, running his hand along the damp paneling.

To his amazement, a section of it moved. He pushed it gently. The floor under his feet lifted and slid forward, sending Bert to the other side of the wall. The panel closed tightly behind him!

In the meantime, on Stage 24, crewmen had raised the neck of the giant Titan crane toward

The panel closed tightly behind Bert!

Nan. Her arms ached as she clung to the wooden beam.

"I can't hold on anymore!" she cried. "Please help me."

Wayne Little had reached the girl by now. Straddling the beam, he grabbed her wrists. "Swing that crane toward us!" he called to the men below.

Nan bit her lips as the small platform atop the crane rose slowly. It stopped short of the girl's dangling feet.

"You're going to have to drop down a little," Wayne told Nan.

"O-Okay," she replied nervously.

"Let your hands slide back."

"I can't. I'll fall."

"You won't fall. Don't look down."

John Kordel and the others watched the pair in silence.

"Go ahead," Wayne coaxed, gripping her arms tightly. Nan released one hand, then the other.

"Easy does it," he said as she lowered herself onto the platform.

Shaking, she sat down. Wayne signaled the operator, who swung the crane back to the floor. The crew gathered around the girl and helped her off the platform.

"Nan!" Flossie exclaimed, running into her sister's arms.

"I'm all right, Floss."

"Are you sure?" John Kordel asked. "What were you doing up there anyhow?"

"I thought I saw somebody on the catwalk after the beam fell."

"Maybe it was just a shadow."

"No, it wasn't," Freddie interrupted. "Bert and I saw him too."

"Where is Bert?" Nan asked.

"He went after the guy."

"But we've got work to do," the director said.

"He told me he would come back as soon as he could."

Kord bristled.

"Maybe we ought to find Bert," Freddie suggested and told his sisters about the van. "I'll show you where it was parked."

The trio went out of the building. There were no visible wheel marks, only a small puddle of liquid. Freddie dipped his finger in it.

"It's oil. I guess the van has a leak," he said.

"What's that?" Nan asked, noticing something on the pavement near the puddle.

Flossie picked it up. "It's a piece of plastic, that's all."

"Let me see it," Nan said.

It was a large white triangle. On the back was stamped "Shark Lagoon." The words, "stunt" and "3 P.M.," were penciled next to it.

"This is supposed to be a tooth from that mechanical shark the studio built for one of its movies," the older girl observed. "I guess it's an advertising gimmick."

"How did it get here?" Flossie asked.

"Do you think the man in the van had it?" Freddie put in.

"Could be," Nan replied. "What time is it, Freddie?"

"Almost quarter to three."

"I think we'll find whoever left this tooth here at Shark Lagoon. Let's go."

A tour bus filled with studio visitors halted in front of the children. "Aren't you the Bobbsey twins?" the operator asked them.

"Yes, we are," Nan said.

"They are starring in a new television series, which will go on the air this fall," the woman announced over her microphone. "Are you excited about your new show?"

The younger twins giggled while Nan made a request. "We'd like to go to Shark Lagoon. Is it far from here?"

"Not at all. As a matter of fact, that's our next stop. Hop on."

As the trio boarded the bus, passengers murmured happily. "May I have your autograph, dear?" one woman asked Flossie. "Is that your twin brother?"

She was eyeing Freddie's monster make-up and black wig.

"Yes, ma'am."

"Does he have to wear that all day long?"

"Mm-hmmmm." She whispered in the woman's ear.

"Oh, I see," she said and told her companion seated next to her. "They're doing a spooky scene in a cave, Mildred. Wait till we tell everybody back home that we met a real star!"

"And there, ladies and gentlemen," interrupted the tour guide, "is famous Shark Lagoon. Now keep your seats, folks, as we pass by. This fish is a lollapalooza. If we're not careful, he could swallow up the entire bus."

It rolled near the edge of the lake.

"I heard something, folks. Just sit back."

Out of the water shot the huge shark, splashing the bus and a few passengers. It opened its jaws wide.

"Ooooowwwwwwweeeeeee!" cried several people.

Flossie and Freddie flinched as the giant mouth closed, then opened again. Nan, unafraid, peered at it.

"One of its teeth is missing," she told the younger twins, excited. "Come on!"

"I bet the studio gives away lots of shark teeth like the missing one," Freddie declared.

Nan did not comment. As the fish dived underwater, she led her brother and sister off the bus. They thanked the driver and headed for the dock area.

"I don't see anybody around here," Flossie said.

They walked to the boathouse, where the front door was slightly ajar. Inside, they noticed partial footprints on the dusty floor and traced them to the stairway. As they made their way to the bottom, they could hear thumping on a wall.

"Bert?" Nan called out. "Is that you?"

Flossie held her brother's hand, squeezing it as the noise grew louder. "I'm s-scared," she confessed.

"I'll protect you, Floss," Freddie said bravely.

"It's coming from behind that wall," Nan said. "Bert?" she called out a second time.

But there was no answer.

The three Bobbseys examined the wall for an opening but found none.

"Maybe it's an animal," Flossie said, hearing the strange sound again.

"Down here?" Nan replied. "Never."

She ran her hands along the lower edge of the partition and noticed a deep crack in the floor boards. She wedged her fingers between them. They moved slightly. Then she felt the wall panel above it.

"Hey, look at this!"

Before the younger twins could catch her, Nan was whisked behind the wall!

"Nan!" Freddie and Flossie cried. "Come back!"

They pushed against the same panel. Within

seconds they joined their sister. "Where are we?" they asked.

"There must be another trick wall around here," the older girl responded. "You check one side and I'll examine the rest. On second thought let's all do it together. I don't want to lose you again."

The three stayed close together and skirted the small empty room. Suddenly Freddie paused.

"Here's something," he declared, tapping his foot on a short wooden strip along the floor.

"It's a latch," Nan said and slid it to one side.

She tugged on the small door beneath it and stared below. "Hello? Is anybody there?" she said.

Again, the children heard thumping.

"It's coming from the other side of this room," Flossie said.

Nan shut the trapdoor. With her sister and brother still close to her, she scanned the opposite wall. Her fingers discovered an indentation in it.

"It's a door!" she exclaimed, and pushed it open.

Bert ran to her. "I'm so glad you're here. How did you know where I was?"

"We didn't. We found a shark's tooth and thought we'd come out to the lagoon," Freddie said quickly.

"How do we get out of here?"

"I don't know. I saw that guy enter this building. He must've come downstairs, but I can't figure out where he went. This place is full of trick panels and walls."

"Do you think he knew you were following him?" Nan asked her brother.

"Now, I think maybe he did. He made sure I got stuck somewhere long enough to let him escape."

As Bert spoke, Flossie leaned against one wall. Part of it swung back, revealing a tunnel. At the end of it was sunlight.

"What are we waiting for?" Bert said, leading the way out.

The four found themselves several feet from the lagoon near a garden surrounding a stone tower. Parked behind a tree was a green van.

"That could be the one I was in!" Bert said.

Nobody was in the driver's seat, and the rear door was not fully latched. The young detectives opened it. Two black eyes greeted them.

"It's a cougar!" Bert cried as the animal bared its fangs and sprang forward.

CHAPTER X

SLIM TIMING

"WATCH out, Bert!" Nan warned as the cougar growled at them.

"He's on a chain," the boy said.

"Even so," Flossie put in, "the chain could break!"

The animal strained against the metal leash, flashing its sharp teeth at the children. Bert shut the door.

"Hey, what's going on over there?" a familiar voice suddenly called out. "Get away from that truck!"

The twins turned around to see several sun reflectors being set up at the base of the stone tower. Slim Willis was running toward the Bobbseys. "Now what are you kids up to?" he questioned them.

"I thought I recognized this van," Bert said.

"Well, what about it?"

"I was mistaken. I'm sorry."

"Ebony has to be kept quiet until we're ready for her. She gets upset when people fuss with her," Slim said.

"We didn't fuss with her," Freddie said.

"I advise you not to either."

"Are you making a movie or a TV show?" Nan asked him.

"We're doing a feature-length film for TV. It's about an old animal trapper who lives in the hills of the Pacific Northwest. The story calls for different kinds of animals. We'll be working with this cougar for a while."

"What about Cheesecake?" Flossie inquired.

"I've got a helper who'll take over on Ebony while I'm on your stage," Slim said.

As the man spoke, Bert noticed a motorcycle parked behind the cameras. "Are you using a stuntman in this scene?" he asked.

"As a matter of fact, we are," Slim muttered. "Look, I've got work to do. If you want to watch us film, be quiet."

The thin man excused himself and joined the director, who was talking to a couple of actors in make-up. Shortly, they stood in front of the cameras and lights. They began their scene.

"Look over there!" Freddie whispered, excited. He pointed to a man who had raced to the tower and began scaling it.

"That's Grady Potts!" Bert said.

"Grady who?" Nan asked, bewildered.

"Potts, Potts," her twin brother repeated.

Freddie dashed to the other side of the tower, out of sight of the cameras and crew.

"Where's he going?" Flossie asked, starting to follow.

"Stay here," Bert called.

Nan darted after her sister and caught her waist. When they were with Bert once again, he revealed the conversation he and Freddie had heard between the man and John Kordel.

"What's Freddie going to do?" Flossie questioned Bert.

"I don't know but I think we ought to stay out of the picture."

Flossie frowned, waiting for her twin brother to come into view. Potts, in the meantime, was climbing the narrow steps that ringed the tower. As he reached the top window, Freddie's dark wig appeared behind it!

"Ohhhh!" Flossie gasped.

Potts opened and shut the window quickly.

"Cut!" the director yelled from below.

"Don't close the window. Climb in! Do you hear me?"

The stuntman nodded.

"Freddie, please come down from there!" Nan mumbled.

Potts backed halfway down the tower.

"Action!" the director called out, signaling the man above to rescale the tower.

"I don't see Freddie's wig anymore," Nan observed.

"Maybe he—"

"Look!" Flossie exclaimed, interrupting Bert.

Potts had entered the tower and several seconds later he emerged through a door at the bottom. He was holding Freddie by his collar!

"Freddie's going to get into trouble now," Nan said.

She and the other Bobbseys ran toward him. The stuntman released his hold on the little boy. "He's not in this script, is he?" Potts snapped at the director.

Slim Willis stepped in. "I told the kids they could watch us quietly," he said. "You'd better get back to Stage Twenty-four if you know what's good for you."

"Not until we ask Mr. Potts a few questions," Bert said. "He tried to run us off—"

"Shmun us, run us," Grady cut off the boy. "I've got work to do. Now scoot."

The director glared at the young detectives. "By the end of the day I have to have one minute of finished film completed. Do you realize how much time this little episode has cost me?"

Grady Potts was holding Freddie by his collar.

Freddie shook his head. "No, sir."

"Plenty," he said. "So if you kids have a bone to pick with Grady, please do it on your own time, not mine. Understand?"

"Yes, sir."

The Bobbseys returned to Stage 24, where the broken beam and shattered glass had been cleared away. New lights stood in place of the damaged ones.

"We can film anytime you're ready," John Kordel said, folding his arms.

When the twins began to tell him all that had occurred, he covered his ears. For the next two hours they talked only about their script. That evening Marcy mimicked the four glum faces before her.

"Why so sad?" she asked Flossie.

"We don't know where Waldo is. We don't know anything about the key. We don't know a lot of things. And Kord is mad at us."

"Kord isn't mad at you," Marcy insisted.

"Yes, he is," Freddie replied. " 'Cause we slowed down protection—"

"Production," Nan corrected him.

Marcy smiled. "I know just what you need."

She took the children's hands and led them to her car. "We're going to the Magic Carpet!"

The Magic Carpet proved to be a small restaurant on the edge of Globe City. Inside, Marcy told the hostess she needed a rug for five. The twins were led to a corner room, where a silvery carpet covered most of the floor. There were no chairs.

"Have a seat," Marcy said to the twins.

Menus floated down on invisible wires in front of each one. Freddie and Flossie giggled at the names of different dishes.

"I'd like a Wing-Ding Chicken," Nan said.

"Me, too," Bert said. "With a vanilla float."

The younger twins took longer to decide but finally Flossie said, "I want a Flying Fruit Salad."

"And I'll have the Magic-Carpet Special," Freddie said.

With that, the carpet lifted the twins into the air!

"Wheeeeeeeeeeeeeeee!" the younger ones laughed.

A voice overhead asked, "Who ordered the Special?"

"I did," Freddie said eagerly.

A tray containing a tall glass of orange drink topped with fresh fruit rose out of the floor toward Freddie. Soon the other trays lifted into place.

"This is fun," Flossie remarked.

Marcy winked at her. When the children had finished eating, the trays lowered into the floor and the carpet slowly swiveled down.

On the way back to the hotel, Bert mentioned the camera and pictures they had had developed. "Could you take us to the police station tomorrow?"

"Certainly," Marcy said.

"When will the extra set of pictures be ready to pick up?" Nan inquired.

"Tomorrow. We can get them on the way to the studio."

The next day Marcy drove the twins to the local police station. "I have an errand to do," she informed them. "But I'll meet you in front of the station as soon as I can."

At the station the Bobbseys introduced themselves to the sergeant on duty.

"What can I do for you?" he asked them.

"A friend of ours found these," they said, and laid the camera and pictures in front of the officer.

He looked at the baby photos, then studied the pictures of the banks. "Who found these?"

"Marcy Sigler," Nan said. "She works for Globe Studios."

"Do you know what these are?" he asked, flashing one of the bank photos at the young detectives.

"Yes, sir. That's why we came to you."

Without saying another word, the policeman pressed a button on his phone. "Has anybody come in for a missing camera?" He paused.

"Who?" He paused again. "Well, tell her to come down here. I want to ask her a few questions.

The man shoved the camera and pictures into a drawer and waved the children away. "Thanks, kids. So long."

"But what about those pictures of the bank?" Freddie asked. "Are you going to try to find out who took them?"

"If we can, but you can't arrest someone for taking a picture."

"We'd like to meet the person who owns the camera," Bert said, hoping the sergeant would give the woman's name.

"To tell the truth, son, I doubt that she has anything to do with the snapshots of the bank."

"He's right," Nan said. "The person who took those wouldn't go to a police station."

"I think you kids have been reading too many mystery stories," the officer commented. "Now don't trouble yourself over this business. Take a trip to Disneyland and have fun."

"But—"

The policeman went back to the paperwork on his desk. Disappointed that he would not discuss the mysterious pictures with them any further, the Bobbseys left. Outside, they looked up and down the street for Marcy. Bert's eyes fell on a large billboard. A jumbo-jet airplane was painted on it.

"Freddie, do you have Waldo's key with you?"

"Mm-hmm," he said and gave it to his brother.

"I think I know where this belongs." He smiled.

"Where?" the little boy asked.

The older detective glanced at the billboard.

"There?" Flossie asked, bewildered.

"Not exactly."

"Come on, Bert. Tell us," Nan urged him.

He twirled the key between his fingers and returned it to Freddie. "I'll show you this afternoon."

CHAPTER XI

COCONUT TROUBLE

BEFORE Bert could say more, Marcy pulled up in front of the police station. "Hi!" she said. "All set to go to the studio?"

"Yup," Freddie replied, following the others into the car.

"We ought to run lines," Nan suggested, pulling her script off the top of the back seat.

"Marcy," Bert interrupted, "can you drive us to the airport after we finish shooting today?"

"Sure. Are you taking a trip? Are the police sending you on a special assignment?" she quipped.

"Nothing like that." Bert chuckled. "I think that key Freddie found on Waldo may fit one of the lockers at Los Angeles Airport."

Freddie removed the key from his pocket and passed it from Flossie to Nan. "I bet you're right, Bert," his twin sister said, then frowned. "But what makes you think it fits a locker in the L.A. airport?"

"Because it suddenly hit me that it looks like the locker key I used when we landed there. Remember how much stuff we carried off the plane? I had to hunt for the studio driver who was supposed to meet us and decided to put my things in a locker."

"Oh, yes," Nan said. "For an amateur detective, you've got a terrific memory!"

"Thanks, sis."

Nan winked at her brother and opened her script. "The scene opens in the living room of Cindy and Peter's home," she said. "The crook has just ransacked some of their furniture. Bert, you start."

"He must've been looking for the coins we found outside the cave," the boy said.

"But how did he break in without any of us seeing him?" his twin asked.

"He has probably been watching our movements for a while. We were in the backyard for at least forty minutes. That's plenty of time to go through a bunch of drawers."

Freddie cleared his throat and pretended to knock on a door. "I forgot to take my house key when I left," he said. "What happened?"

"We had an unwelcome visitor," his older sister said.

"You can say that again," the little boy agreed.

Briefly, the older twins explained who they thought the intruder was and when and how he had entered their home. "So, Adam, what do we do now?" his brother asked.

"Let's have an ice-cream sundae!" interrupted the fourth twin.

"Is your brain always on food, missy?" the boy detectives asked her.

"Not always." As Flossie spoke the line, Marcy entered the studio.

She drove the twins directly to Stage 30, where various rooms of the Baker house had been set up. Inside, the young detectives found crewmen placing cameras and lights opposite the fireplace in the living room. By early afternoon the filming was done, and the Bobbseys returned to their hotel for a nap.

"Who's ready to go to the airport?" Bert asked the other twins an hour later.

"I'm not." Flossie yawned.

"I am," Nan said enthusiastically. "Wake up, Floss. We've got work to do."

The younger girl dragged herself out of bed and rinsed her face with cool water. "I'm coming," she said.

When they all knocked on Marcy's door, she opened it quickly. Her pocketbook was strung over one shoulder and she was holding a large thick book.

"I was just about to call you," she said. "I am going to audition for a great part in a remake of an old movie." If I land it, I'll be on my way to an acting career!"

"What's a remake?" Flossie asked.

"All it means is that the studio is going to film a script that was done a long time ago. There will be some changes in it but it will be the same story."

"And you're going to be in it!" Nan exclaimed happily.

"Maybe, if I'm lucky. I found this script in my mailbox downstairs with a note from Pester Davis."

"Pester Davis?" the twins chorused.

"Yes. It seems that the two young women who went to his office the day we were there saw me. Arlene told Pester she thought I'd be perfect for the role," Marcy said. "I'm really sorry I can't take you to the airport, though."

"Oh, that's okay," Bert said. "We'll take a taxi."

"You know most of the taxis are on strike around here," Marcy pointed out.

"Oh," Nan said. "We'll go some other time then."

"How about tomorrow?" Marcy asked.

The young detectives nodded but were clearly

disappointed. After the young woman stepped into the elevator, Bert spoke. "Maybe we can get someone from the studio to take us," he suggested.

"Who?" his twin sister asked.

"What about Slim Willis?" Freddie suggested.

"Hm. That's an idea," Bert said. "If he's still on the lot, he might be willing to."

The boy dialed the studio phone number. It took several minutes before he heard Slim's voice. When Bert told him why he was calling, Slim coughed.

"I-uh-I'm not going that way. Sorry," he said. "Any other time, though, you want to go to the airport just give me a buzz."

Glumly, Bert said good-by and hung up.

Then he snapped his fingers. "I know—that nice man who met us when we landed. He said if we ever needed to be driven anywhere, he'd be glad to do it."

He found the man's phone number scribbled on a piece of paper in another shirt pocket. Bert called him and in less than twenty minutes the twins were on their way to Los Angeles Airport.

"Please wait for us," the boy requested as they halted in front of the terminal entrance.

"Hey, Bert," Freddie said before they stepped inside the building, "Globe Studios must be making a movie here!"

"There's one of their trucks!" Flossie exclaimed.

"And look who's standing at the airline counter inside," Nan said.

"Who?" Freddie asked.

"Slim Willis."

"Are you sure?" Bert said, staring ahead in disbelief. "He told me he wasn't going this way."

"I guess he didn't want to give us a ride. That's all."

"I bet there's more to it than that," the boy detective commented. "What's the big deal about driving four kids to an airport when you're going there anyway?"

Nan shrugged. As they went inside, they watched Slim disappear into the crowd.

"Forget about him," Bert said. "Let's see if we can find the locker for that key."

They scanned row after row of metal lockers and soon discovered one that matched the number on the key. Bert inserted it in the slot and opened the door. Inside was a cardboard box with the word "coconuts" printed on the front of it. Under that was written "props."

"Coconuts!" exclaimed the younger twins.

"We came all the way here for a box of coconuts?" Nan laughed.

Bert pulled the carton out of the locker and peeked in. "Do you see any coconuts?" he asked, flashing the box in front of the other twins.

"It's just a bunch of papers!" Nan said.

"They look like sketches of a building," Bert observed, "a layout of some sort."

"Coconuts!" the younger twins exclaimed.

"There's something else in the locker too," Flossie said, straining her neck.

A tiny piece of paper lay crumpled in one corner. Nan reached in for it. "I wonder what this is," she said, smoothing it out. "It's got some numbers on it—twenty-five dash one hundred, one hundred dash one thousand, five hundred dash five hundred. What do you think it means?"

"Just about anything," her brother said, "maybe even amounts of money like twenty-five one-hundred bills and so on."

"Ooh—do you think so?" Freddie said.

"We'd better put all of this stuff back," Bert said. "And then we ought to turn the key over to the person in charge of this airport."

He placed the box in the locker and slipped the key in his pants pocket. They headed for the information desk. There they were met by a security officer.

"Please come with me," he said sternly. "You are in big trouble!"

"Trouble?" Nan repeated.

"We haven't done anything wrong," Bert said.

"Taking contents from an airport locker that don't belong to you is pretty serious."

"We didn't do that!" Flossie said.

"We found the key to the locker. We didn't know whom it belonged to," added Freddie.

"So we thought maybe we could find out who lost it by looking inside the locker," Nan explained. "Show him the key, Bert."

"Here it is," the older boy said, digging deep into his pocket. He could not find it. "I know it's here."

He turned the pocket inside out. The stitching at the bottom of it had broken, creating a hole.

"I guess it fell out," Bert said sheepishly.

"Come with me, young man," the security officer said.

CHAPTER XII

TELEPHONE LEAD

BERT and the other young detectives followed the security officer toward a door marked *Personnel Only.*

"We didn't do anything wrong," Freddie insisted. "Honest, we didn't. We found a box of coconuts—"

"Not real ones," Nan said. "The box just said coconuts. There were papers in it and we put it in the locker—"

"And look who's got it now!" Bert interrupted.

Slim Willis was carrying the carton under one arm and rushing toward the exit. The Bobbseys dashed after him.

"Slim!" they called out. "May we talk to you?"

"Hold on!" the security officer exclaimed, running behind the children.

Bert caught up to the man first. "Slim, you've got to help us," he panted breathlessly.

The animal trainer's jaw dropped but he said nothing.

"Please, Mr. Willis," Flossie said.

"How can I help you?" he spoke at last.

"Somebody phoned this security officer that we broke into a locker. That's not true. We used Waldo's key to open it. We didn't know it was your locker," Nan said, eyeing the carton.

"I didn't either. I mean uh—"

"Just a moment," the security officer said. "What was the number of your locker?"

Slim paused. "Uh—1529."

After some more discussion, the officer left the Bobbseys with Slim. Why hadn't Slim recognized the locker key when Freddie showed it to him? they wondered.

"I guess you found the key after I lost it," Bert said.

"If you don't mind, I'm in a hurry," the man replied, turning away briskly.

The young detectives kept up with him. "It was lucky for us we bumped into you," Nan told the animal trainer.

Slim walked faster. "I don't have time to talk now," he said, as the terminal doors slid open, "so don't bother me."

The Bobbseys watched him step into his truck, then headed for their own car.

"Where to?" the driver smiled.

"Back to the hotel, I guess," Nan said.

"Hey, wait a minute!" Bert interjected. "Do you see who's getting out of Slim's truck?"

"It's Pester Davis!" exclaimed Nan.

The others peered at the short, square-shouldered man who had stepped onto the curb. He held a briefcase in one hand and in the other the carton marked "Coconuts." He dropped the box into a litter basket and entered the terminal.

"Come on!" Bert said. "Let's follow him!"

They glanced at the box on the way into the building. It was empty!

"Those papers must be important," Nan commented.

"For him to put them in his briefcase," Flossie said.

"Right," said Freddie.

Unaware he was being followed, Pester stepped into a phone booth. The young detectives squeezed into the next one and pressed their ears against the wall.

"Ouch!" Freddie cried as his twin sister backed onto his toe. "That hurt!"

"Sh!" Nan said. "Do you want Pester to know we're in here?"

They could hear his voice now. "I've got the papers, and I'll be on the five o'clock flight for sure," Pester said. "Are you going to meet us?"

"Us?" Flossie whispered to Freddie. "I wonder who's going with him."

The little boy shrugged as the man continued to speak. "Look, I can't talk any more. What? No. Slim's got to do a job for the studio. He couldn't go with me. Besides, he's expecting a big shipment tomorrow night. Uh-huh. The trucks are rolling in at about eight or so. I'll see you in a while. So long."

The phone clicked off, and the door swung open. The Bobbseys leaned against the back of the booth as Pester Davis passed in front of it.

"I hope he doesn't see us!" Nan mumbled under her breath.

When the man was several feet ahead, the twins emerged.

"I want to get a load of the guy who's traveling with Pester," Bert said.

"So do I," Freddie added.

The young detectives headed for the boarding area of the terminal. It was filled with streams of passengers carrying luggage to the check-in area. Two women, one much older than the other, were strolling two baby carriages. One baby wore a green cap with yellow flowers on it.

"That baby looks awfully familiar," Bert commented, drawing near.

"Especially the hat," Nan said.

Without saying another word to each other, the

"I hope he doesn't see us!" Nan mumbled.

Bobbseys went up to the women. "Excuse me," Nan said, "did either of you lose a camera recently?"

"Or a roll of film," Freddie added.

The gray-haired lady smiled at the children. "As a matter of fact, I did. I lost my camera but I found it. I understand that some children turned it in to the police station. Are you the— But how—"

"We're the ones." Flossie beamed.

"We developed the film," Nan said. "Isn't this the baby you took pictures of?"

"Yes," the woman said. "She's my granddaughter." Pausing, she glanced at the woman next to her.

"You were so sweet to return Mom's camera," she said. "We'd like to give you something as a reward."

"Oh, no," Nan said. "We're glad to know—"

An announcement of a five o'clock flight for San Francisco interrupted the girl. Bert grabbed her hand.

"It was nice meeting you," he said to the women. "Have a nice trip!"

The young detectives hurried ahead to the check-in area. They went through quickly, then scanned the crowd for Pester Davis.

"I don't see him anywhere," Flossie declared. "We should've kept going and not stopped to talk to those ladies."

"But we cleared up one thing, Floss," Nan said. "We learned that the baby pictures were in the camera and those ladies don't look like bank robbers to me. Now if we can just locate the person who took the other set of pictures."

The children walked the length of the corridor, glancing at every gate where passengers were waiting to board.

"There's the San Francisco flight," Bert said, pointing to a line of people forming at a counter. A man in a navy-blue uniform was unlocking a drawer and pulling out sheets of paper and boarding passes.

"Pester said he was leaving at five," Nan commented, glancing up at a small television screen where flight departures and arrivals were printed. "But that doesn't mean he was going exactly at five. There's a four fifty-five leaving for Denver and a four fifty-six to Portland."

"You and Freddie check those gates again. Maybe Pester was hiding behind a newspaper," Bert remarked. "Floss, you come with me."

They stepped into the boarding area for the flight to San Francisco. All of the seats were taken and as latecomers picked up their passes, they crowded in front of those who sat.

"I don't see Pester," Flossie said.

"I do," Bert replied.

He pulled his sister behind the counter and

watched Pester move toward a man in a green turtleneck sweater. He bent down and whispered something in the man's ear. The other one, poker-faced with sharp features, nodded.

"Stick close to me, Floss," Bert said. "Let's get as near him as we can without being seen."

"Okay."

They slid behind a group of people at the ticket desk and followed several who were walking in Pester's direction. Three men with garment bags stopped near him. Hidden by the bags, Bert and Flossie listened closely to the pair on the other side.

"Those Bobbseys are real snoops. They're poking into our business," Pester said.

"Oh, yeah?"

"Of course, they're just kids."

The young detectives bristled.

"We've got more important things to think about—"

The men's voices were drowned out for a moment by a flight announcement. "Flight twelve to San Francisco will be delayed ten minutes," the voice said.

"Whew!" Pester said. "That's all we need—"

"What did you do about Marcy?" the other man asked now.

"I lined up an audition for her. I thought if I kept her busy she wouldn't be available to drive those kids around today. I didn't want them to bug me again. But Slim says he saw them around here—"

Bert could feel his face redden. A second flight announcement came over the loudspeaker and cut off Pester's voice. "Passengers please have your boarding passes ready to show at the gate."

"We'd better go," Bert told his sister.

The men with the garment bags reached into their pockets as a plump woman crushed her tote bag against the children and pushed them forward. They stood face to face with Pester Davis.

"Where did you come from?" he snarled at the Bobbseys.

CHAPTER XIII

THE BUBBLETIME FLOOD

PESTER Davis's eyes pierced through Bert and Flossie as he talked. "What are you doing here?"

"We—uh—we—" Bert stammered. "We have to go. Bye."

He and Flossie broke through the crowd behind them and raced down the corridor. They passed Nan and Freddie.

"We found Pester!" Bert told them quickly.

"Why are you running?" Nan replied, darting after him.

"Come back here!" a voice bellowed at the end of the hallway.

Freddie turned his head but did not stop. "It's Pester! He's chasing us!"

"Just keep moving!" Bert exclaimed.

They skirted the check-in area and aimed for the terminal exit. For an instant the older twins glanced back. The final announcement of the San Francisco flight came over the loudspeaker.

"Flight twelve is now ready for departure," the voice said.

Pester Davis came to a halt. He paused, then returned to the gate.

"Wow!" Freddie exclaimed. "He looked really angry."

"What happened?" Nan asked her brother.

"I'll tell you in the car."

As they left the building, the twins noticed that Slim's truck was gone. They asked their driver if he recalled when it had left.

"Oh, almost right after you went inside."

"That's good," Bert said. "Then Slim didn't pay attention to us when we followed Pester."

"Not necessarily," Nan said. "Maybe he just decided to leave, that's all. Now please tell Freddie and me why Pester was running after us. What's going on?"

As the driver headed the car for the twins' hotel, Bert and Flossie repeated the conversation they had overheard between the talent agent and the man in green.

"There is something very fishy going on," Bert said.

"And Pester doesn't want us to know about it," Flossie joined in.

At the hotel, the twins found Marcy in her room. Her eyes were red and puffy.

"Hi!" She smiled, but the children knew she had been crying.

"What's the matter, Marcy?" Flossie asked, putting her arms around the young woman's shoulder.

"Oh, nothing." She gulped.

"How did your audition go?" Bert asked.

"It didn't," she said tearfully.

"It didn't?" Nan repeated.

Marcy shook her head. "I didn't get the part," she said. "They told me I was too cute." She laughed a little. "I guess they were looking for a sourpuss."

Flossie made a face. "Like this?" She giggled.

"You'd be perfect!" Marcy exclaimed happily. "Oh, I almost forgot. You've got a new assignment."

"We do?" Nan asked.

"It seems that Caramel and Chester Potts were supposed to be in a bubble-bath commercial. They can't do it and wondered if you could take their place."

The twins looked at each other. "I love bubble bath!" Flossie said.

"So do I!" Freddie added.

"But I think Caramel and Chester were hoping you and Nan could stand in for them," Marcy turned to Bert.

He frowned. "Oh, that's kid stuff."

"Come on, Bert," Nan said. "It'll be fun."

"When are we supposed to do this wonderful thing?" Bert asked in disgust.

"Tomorrow morning. It won't take long," Marcy said.

"Can't we be in it too?" Flossie asked.

"I don't know, honey. But I'll find out for you. Okay?"

The little girl nodded, excited.

"Now tell me where you've been this afternoon. I came back to the hotel expecting to find you all sacked out. I gather you found a ride to the airport."

The twins told the young woman about their experiences at the terminal. Her eyes grew wide. "Oh, my. Oh, my," she gasped.

"Don't worry about us," Freddie said bravely. "We're used to this sort of stuff."

The next morning she awakened the young detectives early and delivered them to a small building. It was much like the sound stage they worked in at the studio. There were lights and cameras set up around a low platform. On it was a white-porcelain counter lined with bottles of pink liquid.

"How do you do?" a cheerful man addressed

the twins. "I'm your director, Sidney Gunther. And you must be Bert and Nan Bobbsey."

Freddie and Flossie edged closer but the man ignored them at first. "Mr. Gunther, can we— can I take a bubbly bath?" the little girl asked, bouncing up and down.

"Hmm," the director paused. "I think I will make a change in the script. Okay, Flossie, you and Nan get behind that counter."

"Oh, phooey," Freddie said, disappointed to be left out. Bert relaxed and grinned.

Mr. Gunther explained what would happen step by step. "You don't have too many lines to say. Just remember how much you love Bubbletime Bath and keep smiling!"

The girls changed into strapless bathing suits, and towels were wrapped around them. Shortly the director waved his hand at a cameraman and said, "Action."

"I *love* Bubbletime Bath!" Flossie exclaimed as clear soapy bubbles rose from behind the counter.

"You will too!" Nan said, looking straight into the camera.

Overhead two voices giggled mischievously. "No, you won't!" one declared and dumped a pail of ice-cold water over the girls.

"Yikes!" Nan cried, swallowing a mouthful. Flossie squealed, shutting her eyes. "Stop!"

The director gazed up at the small platform

"Stop!" Flossie squealed.

jutting out from a wall. "Who's up there?" he asked. "Come down here this minute."

There were more giggles, then the sound of footsteps running down a back stairway. Bert and Freddie dashed toward it with Sidney Gunther close behind.

"Caramel and Chester, what on earth—" he boomed out when they reached the bottom steps.

"We didn't mean it—" the girl said, hunching up her shoulders.

"I think you owe me an explanation and these young ladies an apology!" the director scolded them.

They turned around, their heads hanging.

"You told me you were too busy to work today," Mr. Gunther exclaimed. "Now what's all this about?"

"We—" Chester began, clearing his throat.

"They wanted to put us down," Bert said, "because they think we took their parts in our new TV series. Right?"

The Potts twins nodded slowly.

"I've got a good name for you kids," Gunther declared. "Pitts!"

The children flinched. "We're sorry," Caramel said.

"I'm not!" Chester announced. "They did steal our job!"

"We did not!" Freddie exclaimed.

"Did not!" Flossie added as Nan continued to dry her curls.

"That's what our agent told us," Caramel said quietly.

"Who's your agent?" Nan asked.

"Pester Davis."

"Pester Davis?"

The Bobbseys froze. Had Pester deliberately tried to cause trouble between the children? Or was he just trying to save face as an agent?

"Pester is one of the best agents around town," Chester observed.

"And if anyone could have gotten us parts on *The Young Detectives* he could!" Caramel insisted.

Sidney Gunther cleared his throat. "I don't mean to disillusion you kids," he said, "but Pester's reputation as an agent has slipped a little."

"What do you mean, Mr. Gunther?" Caramel queried.

"Well, he seems preoccupied with other things. I had lined up a cereal commercial for you last week, but Pester said he was too busy. He asked me if there was anything you could handle this week instead. That's when I told him about Bubbletime. I didn't know how our client would feel about a boy advertising for bubblebath. To my amazement, the client said, 'Kids are kids!'

"I wouldn't have told you all of this," the director went on, "except that I don't think you are being fair to the Bobbseys."

Caramel and Chester were too stunned to say anything at first.

"See?" Freddie said to them.

"I'm sorry," Caramel apologized.

"Okay, I didn't mean to dump water on you," Chester added.

Nan, still dripping, broke into a smile. "At least I had a bathing suit on," she said.

"Well, now that we're all friends again," the director put in, "may we get back to work. Since you girls are all wet, I'm afraid Caramel and Chester will have to do the commercial."

"That's fine with us," Nan said.

Flossie pouted most of the way back to the hotel. "I want to take a bubble bath," she said.

"I'd say you got bubble soaked!" Marcy quipped after hearing about the morning's events.

"Cheer up, Floss," Nan said. "You can take a bubble bath tonight. Mr. Gunther gave me this." She pulled a small bottle of the lotion out of her jacket pocket.

"Oh, goody!" Flossie grinned.

As the children stepped into the lobby of the hotel, Bert's eyes fell on a pile of newspapers in front of a small stand. He picked up one of the papers and dropped a few coins on the counter.

"What's the big news?" Nan asked.

"Look!" Bert exclaimed.

The younger twins stared at the bold black print in the headline. It read:

THIRD BANK ROBBERY IN SAN FRANCISCO AREA
BANDITS STEAL MILLION

CHAPTER XIV

SURPRISING DISCOVERY

"May I read the newspaper after you're finished with it, Bert?" Nan asked him.

"Sure."

"Who stole the money from the bank?" Flossie inquired.

"Is that a picture of the bank?" Freddie added, scanning the photo next to the article.

"Yes." Bert paused, then began to read the story aloud. " 'Late last night thieves broke into the San Francisco City Bank and stole more than one million dollars in cash, coins, and valuables, a spokesman for the bank reported. "There was no sign of disturbance—no broken glass, no explosion. The bank vault was open when I got to work," said the man, who did not give his name. "Whoever robbed us knew the layout of our building—knew where every corner, hallway, and desk was." '

" 'Police are working round the clock to catch the thieves before another bank robbery occurs.

" 'This marks the third such theft in the past month. Banks throughout the state of California are tightening security.' "

"Gee, I hope those fellows don't decide to move to Los Angeles," Marcy commented. "My bank account already has a big dent in it!"

"Do you think those pictures—the extra set— are ready yet?" Bert asked the young woman.

"Maybe. We can stop by the film lab on the way to Stage Thirty if you like."

"I would."

"Want to compare those shots with this news-paper photo?" Nan interjected.

"Yes."

"But how did a bank robber in San Francisco lose a roll of film in Globe City?" Freddie put in.

"I don't understand that either," Flossie said.

"Well, I don't really have any terrific theories yet," Bert said.

The Bobbseys had about an hour to rest before going to Globe City Studios. Each one thought about the strange way Slim Willis had acted, the box of papers, and Pester Davis's reaction when he saw Bert and Freddie.

"I've been trying to figure out why Slim carried that box to his truck," Bert said to Freddie while they were stretched out on their beds.

"Because he wanted to give those papers to Pester," Freddie replied.

"True, but why didn't Pester just go to the locker himself and take the papers?"

"Because he didn't want to be seen putting them in his briefcase?"

"That's the only reason I can think of."

"But I don't see what the big deal is about those papers," the little boy went on. "They weren't anything special."

"Maybe they were. They must be."

"It was lucky for Slim he found the locker key. Otherwise, he wouldn't have been able to get the box," Freddie said.

"I guess he figured an airport security man could open it," Bert said. "Anyway, he must've recognized the number on the key when you showed it to him. Why didn't he tell us it belonged to him?"

"I don't know. I guess he wanted to keep it a secret."

"I'd like to go out to his house tonight and see what those trucks are bringing him," Bert said.

"What if Slim catches us on his property?" Freddie replied, excited.

"He won't."

Bert set his alarm and drifted off to sleep. His

brother, however, stared at the ceiling. Was there a connection between the pictures they had found and the bank robberies in San Francisco? What kind of scheme, if any, were Slim and Pester mixed up in? Would the Bobbseys ever figure out the answers? Freddie dozed off, wondering.

When the buzzer on the alarm sounded, both boys snapped their eyes open. They met Nan, Flossie, and Marcy in the hallway and headed for her car.

"Did you have a good snooze?" the young woman asked the children.

Freddie and Flossie yawned. "I did," the little girl said, " 'cept I kept thinking about Slim and Pester."

"So did we," Freddie noted. "We want to go out to Slim's house tonight?"

"Tonight?" Marcy blinked. "Is that a wise idea?"

"We'll be careful," Bert promised. "Would you—"

"Drive you," Marcy finished.

"At least as far as the corner of his street. We'll walk the rest of the way," Bert went on.

"We don't want Slim to see us," Nan said.

Marcy rolled her eyes. "I have a feeling I ought to say no."

"Oh, please, pretty please," Flossie begged.

"Okay, okay, you win."

"Yippee!" Freddie cried happily.

On the way to the studio the eager detectives discussed their plans for the evening. "You should be finished filming before five or six," Marcy said, as she pulled up in front of a low building at the edge of the studio lot. "Here's the film lab. I'll be out in a jiffy."

She hurried inside and reappeared shortly with an envelope. "You're in luck," she told the Bobbseys. "Your pictures were ready."

"Great," Nan said.

While Marcy drove the children to Stage 30, they scanned the photographs closely. Freddie took a few in his hand and studied one in particular.

"Do you see some writing on this one?" he said, showing a picture to Nan.

"Where?"

"Right here on the glass door of the bank."

"Let me see it," Flossie said, glancing at the photo.

"I don't see any writing," Nan replied at first. "Oh, wait a minute. Now I do. You mean the reflection of some letters on the glass. I see a t,a,g and an n,e,d. It must be part of a sign of some sort, opposite the door. If we were looking at the sign itself the letters would be reversed."

"I wonder what it means," Flossie said as they reached the stage entrance.

Bert put the pictures in his pocket and followed the others inside. There a car was parked

"Do you see some writing in the picture?" Freddie said.

in front of a small movie screen. A film of moving traffic played across it.

"I want to run through this scene quickly so fix your make-up and be on the set in fifteen minutes."

"Okay, Kord," Bert replied, laying his script on a chair.

He and the others glanced at their lines briefly just before stepping into the car.

"We're going awfully slow," Flossie giggled, watching the vehicles whiz alongside on the screen.

"Not too slowly," the director interrupted. "You're in a taxi and you've just spotted the jeep you saw in that old garage."

The twins nodded.

"Action!" John Kordel said.

"Cindy, isn't that the jeep with the New Jersey license plates?" was Bert's first line.

"It sure looks like the same one."

"He's heading toward the caves!" was Freddie's line.

"Let's follow him!" his twin sister exclaimed.

The car now bounced gently.

"Cut!" the director said. "All right, Bob, you take the driver's seat."

The camera swung toward the actor who slid behind the steering wheel. Again the director said, "Action."

"How far do you kids want to go on this highway?" he asked.

"Just as far as that jeep ahead will take us," the older boy said.

"Not to the Golden Gate Bridge, I hope," quipped the man who played the taxi driver.

"Golden Gate Bridge!" Nan exclaimed. "That's it! D-e-n-g-a-t--"

"Cut!" the director shouted. "That's not in the script!"

Nan bit her tongue. "I'm sorry," she apologized, "but I just realized something."

Bert winked at her. "You're right!" he whispered. "I'm positive those pictures were taken in San Francisco!"

"Ooh, Nan!" Flossie bubbled. "How 'citing!"

Freddie beamed too.

The twins said no more about their discovery until they finished filming. Then Freddie asked his brother, "What do we do about these pictures?"

"Shouldn't we return to the police station?" Nan asked when they were back in their hotel.

Instead, Bert telephoned the sergeant on duty and reported their news. He thanked the boy and simply said he would take a second look at the photographs.

Hanging up, Bert shrugged. "I guess it's routine to him."

Later that evening the twins changed into

plain, dark shirts and slacks. Freddie and Flossie wore the same brown outfits, while Nan and Bert dressed in green. As planned, Marcy drove them to the edge of the road where the Willis home stood.

"The moon's bright tonight," Nan commented. "I hope nobody sees us."

"Just keep close to the trees," Bert told her. "Marcy, will you wait for us right here?"

"Anything you say," she replied. "Are you sure you'll be all right?"

"Sure we're sure. Don't worry."

"Oh, I'll worry," she said, letting the engine of her car idle while the twins got out.

There was only the rustle of leaves blowing gently in the breeze and the soft buzzing of locusts. Quietly, the twins walked up the road. The first house they passed had no lights on.

"Boy, it's dark around here!" Freddie shivered. Suddenly, something furry darted across his feet. "Yaaah—" he started to exclaim aloud.

Bert clamped a hand over the little boy's mouth. "Do you want to wake everybody up?" he cautioned.

"N-No-oh," Freddie stammered when Bert let go.

On the other side of the road a small kitten arched its back and meowed. Then it disappeared into the woods.

"Scaredy cat!" Flossie giggled at her twin.

In the distance, two large headlights loomed toward them. "It's a truck!" Bert declared. "Maybe it's the one Slim is waiting for. Get back!"

The twins hid behind a broad tree trunk and waited for the vehicle to turn into the Willis driveway.

"Well, that's not it," Nan said, as the truck droned past them. "Come on."

They turned back for a moment. Marcy had shut off her car lights. But in the moonlight they could see her watching them. Bert took Flossie's hand and led her to the edge of the Willis property. One lamp flickered in the living-room window. Slim was pacing back and forth. He glanced outside.

"Duck!" Bert ordered.

The young detectives dropped behind a row of bushes. At the same time, another pair of headlights appeared on the road.

"This is it!" Bert whispered as a van slowed up in front of the Willis home and backed into the driveway.

CHAPTER XV

DOLLAR DELIVERY

As the truck pulled into the driveway of the Willis house, the Bobbseys kept low behind the bushes. Slim and his wife opened the front door quickly and rushed outside.

"Where have you been?" Slim asked the driver.

"That's the guy we saw with Pester!" Bert muttered under his breath.

"He's got the same green sweater on," Freddie observed.

The boys became quiet when the truck driver spoke. "I've been on the road since last night. I had to take a detour around Monterey. You're lucky I'm here at all."

"Okay, okay," Slim said. "Let's get rolling."

The driver gunned the engine and pulled the truck behind the house. The animal trainer and his wife walked alongside the vehicle.

"Keep going," Slim said, waving his hand at the driver. "Back, back. Okay, stop."

In a flash the twins raced across the front lawn to a low hedge that bordered the front porch. Hearing the crunch of footsteps on the gravel driveway, they ducked behind the hedge.

Bert's heart beat fast as he took a deep breath. "Let's go!" he whispered.

"No, Bert!" Nan said, tugging on his arm. "They'll see us!"

He eased toward the corner of the house and peered around it. Slim had turned on a light in the shedlike building behind, and the driver was opening the rear door of the truck.

"That's strange," Bert thought, studying the side of the truck. "There's some writing on it but it's all covered up with paint."

He and Nan stood close together as cartons stamped with the word "Props" were slid off the vehicle and carried inside.

"Hurry up!" Slim told the driver. "Get them all inside fast!"

"Look, I'm doing the best I can."

The men argued a bit while the twins watched.

"Work first, talk later," Mrs. Willis interrupted them.

She jumped up on the truck and began shoving a large carton toward the men. "Don't you do that, Edith. Let Jimmy. That's what he's getting paid for." Slim growled.

When all of the boxes were in the coop, the trio went into the house. "I wonder how long they'll stay inside," Bert said.

"I'm scared!" Flossie cried.

"I want to see what's in those boxes," Nan cut in.

"Me too!" Freddie exclaimed.

"It looks like a studio truck," Bert observed, "but I bet there isn't one prop on it!"

"What'll we do?" Flossie asked.

"You and Freddie run back to Marcy. Nan and I will check out the coop, then join you. Wait for us."

"But I want to go with you," Freddie pleaded.

"You stick with Flossie. There's no sense in all of us going in that shed," Bert said.

The little boy pouted but said no more. He took his sister's hand. When the coast was clear, they leaped across the lawn and headed for the car at the end of the road.

"Are you with me?" Bert asked his twin.

"All the way," Nan said.

They listened for a moment. A window was open in the kitchen. Through it they could hear voices.

"It sounds like Slim is talking on the phone to somebody," Nan said. "But I can't quite figure out what he's saying."

"We'd better make a run for it now," Bert said.

The pair dashed across the gravel and slipped past the truck. The door of the shed was ajar. Bert glanced at the open kitchen window. Jimmy and the Willises were seated at a table with the phone between them. Bert squeezed Nan's hand and moved ahead.

On the wall was a map of California. The major cities, including San Diego, Los Angeles, and San Francisco, were circled in red. There was a long wooden table under the map. The boxes were piled in front of it.

Without saying a word to each other, the twins hurried to the boxes. They were sealed shut with strong nylon tape. Bert slipped his fingers under one edge of the carton and pulled hard.

"I ca-n't o-pen i-it!" he said. "Help me, Nan!"

She had tried to undo another box without success. Now she wedged her fingers alongside her brother's and tugged on the tape.

"It's coming!" she said, gritting her teeth.

"Wait a minute! I hear something!" Bert interrupted.

They froze. What would they do if they were caught?

"It's nothing," Bert said after a moment and yanked one more time on the carton.

The tape loosened.

"Come on!" Nan muttered.

She tore at the stripping. Finally it came off.

"Oh!" the young detectives gasped, as they opened the box. "It's money!"

"And lots of it!" Bert exclaimed.

He dug through the box and pulled out bunches of dollar bills. "We've got to tell the police!" he said.

"Let's get out of here!" Nan replied.

As she spoke, the back door of the house opened and closed. "Quick, hide!" Bert exclaimed.

He stuffed the bills in the carton, flipped it shut, and pointed to a couple of small covered barrels in a corner. "In there!" he said.

"There?" Nan winced, afraid she would not fit into the container.

The voices grew louder, causing the girl to get into the barrel as fast as she could. She squeezed her arms close to her and bent down. Bert slipped the top over her, then got into the other barrel.

"Oh, I bet they find us!" Nan worried.

The shed door opened. Through cracks in the barrels, the young detectives could see Slim and Jimmy. They did not seem to pay attention to the box with the loose tape.

"Oh, I hope they don't come over here!" Bert thought.

"It's money!" The young detectives gasped.

The men checked the map. "A million's not bad for one night's work!" Jimmy said.

"Don't congratulate yourself yet," cautioned Slim. "We have to get this money into Mexico first. Then it's ours for sure!"

"Oh, we'll get it there. After all, who's going to question the fact that I'm carrying studio props for a new movie we're making down there?"

"I've got to hand it to Pester," Slim said.

"Pester! It wasn't his idea to use the studio for our business," Jimmy said.

"I know, I know. But he had a lot to do with the smoothness of everything."

Bert's and Nan's ears burned as they listened to the men's conversation. "Should we count the money here?" Jimmy asked.

"Of course. Why do you think you have ten fingers?" the other man snickered.

"Very funny."

"Hey, look at this box," Slim said. "Were you planning to dip into the funds before all of us got our share?"

"Are you crazy?"

"Well, how do you explain the broken tape. That stuff's like iron. Somebody snapped it."

The twins held their breaths.

"Count it for yourself. Every dollar is there. I didn't touch one."

Slim dumped the carton on the table and began counting the contents. When he was done, he smiled at his partner. "You're okay, buddy. It's all here, just the way it's supposed to be," he said.

"You know, I've got a feeling we're being watched," Jimmy declared.

He walked toward the barrels. Nan shut her eyes tight, praying he would not uncover them. "Do you see what I see?" he asked Slim, pointing to a tiny fold of Nan's shirt that protruded through the crack in her barrel.

Nan now stared at the man's shoes facing her. Like lightning, he pulled off the top of the barrel. "Well, if it isn't the little lady from the airport!" he said.

Bert jumped up from his hiding place. The barrel cover clattered to the floor as he tried to escape. But Jimmy's strong arms gripped him tightly.

"Now where do you think you're going?" he sneered.

"Let go of me!" Bert shouted.

"Don't hurt my brother!" Nan begged.

Slim held her in tow, saying, "Nobody is going to get hurt."

"Who knows you came here?" Jimmy questioned the twins.

"Nobody." Bert said quickly.

"Oh, is that so? What about your brother and sister?"

"Where are they?" Slim joined in.

"They're not here."

"Well, we can see that for ourselves."

Jimmy whispered something to his companion, then told the children to get back in the barrels.

"What are you going to do to us?"

"You're going to take a little trip right now," Slim said, setting the barrel covers in place again.

"Where?" Nan asked, her voice muffled by the wood.

The men did not answer. They wrapped the tape from the opened box across the tops of the containers. "That should do it," Slim said.

"We'll count the money later," the other man added.

They carried each barrel onto the truck, then latched the rear door. The twin detectives pushed up against the tightened lids. They would not budge.

"We'll never get out of here!" Nan thought anxiously as the truck rumbled forward.

Undaunted, Bert rocked his weight against the side of the container. It toppled a bit, then turned over.

"Oh!" Nan screamed, seeing the barrel roll in front of her toward the door.

The truck began to climb a hill. The barrel rolled back, spinning the boy from one end of the vehicle to the other. His shoulders and arms ached as the barrel crashed against the door a second time. The latch loosened.

"Oh, no!" Nan cried as the barrel rested by the opening. "If we go uphill, Bert will roll off the truck!"

CHAPTER XVI

CAUGHT!

As the truck swerved around a corner, Bert's barrel slid to the side of the floor, and the tape across the cover split.

"Bert, are you all right?" his sister cried.

There was no response at first, then a low groan. The boy detective squirmed out of the container and stumbled to his feet.

"Now I know what it feels like to be a yo-yo," Bert said, shaking his head.

He swayed dizzily toward Nan and tore the tape off the top of the barrel she was in. She rocked to her feet as the truck took another sharp turn.

"Maybe we can jump off," Bert suggested.

He pushed against the rear door. The latch slipped out of the catch, allowing the door to swing free. The twins clung to the sides of the truck and peered out into the darkness. Street lights spaced far apart shone dimly through the trees.

"I don't see any houses, do you?" Nan asked her brother.

"Nope. But there must be some somewhere."

The truck bounced over the rough road and seemed to gain speed. "Oh, Bert, what'll we do? We can't jump," Nan said nervously.

The barrel she had been in wobbled, then overturned. It rolled toward the door.

"Watch it!" Bert exclaimed.

His sister leaped aside as he reached for the inside handle. But he was too late. The barrel slipped between him and the open door. It crashed on the pavement and tumbled into the ditch. "I hope those guys didn't hear that," Bert said, shutting the door.

Meanwhile, Freddie and Flossie had waited for their brother and sister in Marcy's car.

"They've been gone an awfully long time," Marcy declared. "Are you sure they're all right?"

"They're doing some big detective work," Flossie stated.

"I think we should've stayed with them," Freddie said. "They probably need help."

"Well, I'm going up to the Willis house to find them," the young woman declared, starting her car.

"Oh, don't do that!" Flossie begged.

"Floss," said Freddie, "that's a good idea."

"Huh?"

"Marcy can drive past the house and let us off if nobody's around to see us."

"I'm not letting you out of my sight," Marcy commented.

She drove slowly up the road.

"Hey, the truck's gone!" Freddie exclaimed, as the Willis house and driveway came into view.

"It's pretty quiet," Flossie said. "And I don't see Bert and Nan anywhere."

Marcy pulled in front of the house and stopped. "You stay here," she told the young detectives and got out of her car.

As she went up the front steps, the living-room light turned off. "Mrs. Willis, Slim," she called but no one came.

The Bobbseys watched her a few moments, then Freddie said, "Come on, let's go."

"But Marcy told us not to leave the car," Flossie replied.

"Do you want to find Nan and Bert or don't you?"

" 'Course I do."

"Then, come on!"

While Marcy looked in the front window, the small children slipped out of the car and ran behind the house to the old shed. It was pitch-black.

"I don't want to go in there!" Flossie told Freddie.

"I'll protect you," he whispered.

The little girl gulped as he pressed against the doorknob. Freddie took one step inside and gazed around the room.

"There's just a bunch of boxes," he remarked.

"Are you sure?" Flossie asked, afraid.

"Mm-hmm."

Flossie followed her twin toward the cartons piled under the table. They gasped when they saw several stacks of dollar bills in an open box.

"Look!" Flossie exclaimed, bending close to it. "Here's Nan's comb!"

The tiny blue hair comb lay on the floor where it had fallen earlier. It was cracked.

"Those men must've caught Nan and Bert!" Freddie exclaimed.

As he spoke, the door behind the twins creaked shut. "You children really ought to behave yourselves," Mrs. Willis said.

Freddie and Flossie jumped. They tried to run past her but she flattened herself against the door and spread her arms around them.

"Where's Marcy?" Flossie cried.

"Now, don't you worry about her," the woman snapped.

"Here's Nan's comb!" Flossie exclaimed.

"What did you do with my sister and brother?" Freddie questioned.

"They're being taken care of—"

"Where are they?" Flossie sobbed.

Edith Willis's face broke into an evil smile. "Now wouldn't you like to know." She cackled.

In the meantime, the truck on which Nan and Bert had been imprisoned began climbing along a steep ravine.

"He's going a lot slower," Bert said to his twin sister. "Maybe we can make a break now."

He held the rear door open wide enough to scan the terrain. There were lots of trees at the foot of the ravine, and across the road a mountain of them loomed high. The twins stared at each other. Then, together they leaped off the truck. Nan tripped as she fell and twisted her foot slightly. Bert helped her up.

"Okay?" he asked, as the truck came to a halt.

"They'll see us!" Nan said anxiously.

She gripped her brother's arm. In spite of the pain in her foot, she ran with him down the edge of the ravine. Jimmy stepped out of his side of the truck and dashed to the rear.

"You're right, Slim. They're gone!" the twins heard the driver say.

They hid behind an outcrop of rock where a broad tree trunk lay in front of it. Bert squeezed his sister's hand as the men's voices became louder.

"Don't breathe!" he whispered in Nan's ear.

Her heart pounded as Slim said, "We'll find 'em. They couldn't have gone far."

"But they're smart kids," the other man reminded his companion.

They stopped speaking for a long while.

"Where'd they go?" Nan wondered fearfully. "I wish they would keep talking so I could tell where they were."

Bert did not dare say a word to his sister. "They could be on the other side of this rock," he thought unhappily.

Then, suddenly, Jimmy's voice cut through the stillness. "I give up," he said. "Let's get moving."

"He's gone toward the truck again," Nan concluded. "But where is Slim?"

"Just a minute," said the wily animal trainer.

Nan panicked. "He's about a foot away!"

She braced herself against the rock while Bert glanced behind him for an escape route. The ravine dropped down several feet before it leveled again. In the moonlight he could see small boulders below him. He nodded at Nan to look in the same direction.

"Can you make it?" he mouthed the words.

She shrugged, but hearing Slim's footsteps close by, she shook her head, yes. Carefully, the pair edged away from their hiding place.

At the same time, Freddie and Flossie were trying to figure out how to escape from Edith Willis. "You leave us alone!" Flossie exclaimed.

She stomped on Mrs. Willis's toe. "Ouch!" the woman cried, letting go of the children.

They slipped under her arm and yanked on the handle of the shed door. "Hurry, Freddie!" his small sister screamed as the woman hopped forward.

He jiggled the handle from one side to the other but the door would not budge. "Oh, no you don't!" Mrs. Willis said, pouncing on Flossie.

"Help!" Flossie screeched.

Freddie stepped on the woman's other big toe.

"Why, you—" She said, releasing her grip on Flossie.

Quickly, Freddie turned the handle again and crashed against the door. "It's stuck!" he said. "It's stuck. It's stuck!"

To his amazement, the door flung inward. Pester Davis stood before him. "It's not stuck." He grinned.

The young twin backed away slowly as the man moved toward him. Edith Willis clamped her hands on Flossie's shoulders. Freddie did not take his eyes off Pester.

"I just flew in," he told Mrs. Willis and grabbed hold of Freddie's collar.

"It's a good thing," the woman replied. "I've got my hands full."

"I can see that. Where are the other two?" the talent agent questioned.

"Slim and Jimmy have them."

"Good."

Unaware that their younger brother and sister had been trapped in the Willis shed, Nan and Bert worked down the ravine toward a boulder. It rested in the middle of two trees.

"There's a road down there!" Nan observed, wincing a bit from the throb in her foot.

"Can you make it?"

"Sure."

In the distance, they could hear the race of the truck engine as it started upward again. "At least they're gone," Nan sighed. "If we only knew where we were, though."

Teasing, Bert held up his index finger. "Wind's from the North. We're traveling due south," he said brightly.

"In the middle of the night." Nan frowned and added, "Just think I could be in my nice warm hotel room, reading my script."

"Stop dreaming," Bert said.

"Are we really going south?"

"Your guess is as good as mine. But I know one thing. If we keep heading in one direction we are bound to come out somewhere."

"Brilliant, brother."

The two detectives soon reached the narrow

road that stretched toward a valley dotted with lights. "Civilization!" Nan remarked. "Now all we need to find is a policeman."

"And a splint for your foot."

Nan leaned on Bert's shoulder as she hobbled along quickly on the grass-lined pavement. The rear lights of a car disappeared around the bend ahead of the twins.

"There's another car coming," Nan observed. "Maybe we can get a ride to the next town."

Bert waved his hand at the oncoming vehicle. The driver flashed his high beams on the pair, blinding them.

"Oh-oh," Bert gasped, recognizing the truck.

He pulled Nan out of its path as it screeched to a fast stop. Slim and Jimmy leaped toward the boy and girl.

CHAPTER XVII

PLANE END

"So you thought you could get away from us!" Slim Willis said with an evil grin.

He and Jimmy reached for Bert first. "Let go of me!" the boy exclaimed, feeling the men's fingers dig into his arm.

Slim shoved Bert into the back of the truck while Jimmy grabbed Nan.

"I'm not going. I'm not going!" she screamed. "You can't make me!"

The muscular man gripped her wrists tightly and pulled her toward Bert. Nan felt a twinge of pain in her foot as she tried to hold her ground but could not.

"Okay. You asked for it!" Jimmy snapped.

He scooped her up in his broad arms and flung her into the truck against Bert. The men shut the doors and latched them securely.

"Oh, Bert!" Nan cried. "It's all my fault."

"That's a dumb thing to say. It's nobody's fault."

"Well, if I hadn't twisted my foot, we could've gotten away from those men."

The young detectives sank into silence as the truck sped along the deserted road. In a while it slowed down but did not stop.

"We must be going through that town we saw just before they caught up with us," Bert remarked.

The screech of brakes told the Bobbseys they had arrived at their destination. Where were they? Would they have another chance to escape from Slim and Jimmy? they wondered. The back door of the truck opened.

"Get out!" Slim snarled at the pair.

Without speaking, Bert helped Nan to her feet and led her slowly to the edge of the truck. "Can you walk okay?" he asked his sister.

"Come on. Come on!" Jimmy interrupted. "Quit talking and move."

He started to get into the truck.

"She hurt her foot," Bert told the men.

"So what?" Jimmy replied, grabbing Nan's arm.

Bert bristled but did not say a word as Nan stepped down.

"Where are we?" she asked, glancing at a row of buildings next to the truck.

"We're at Globe Studios!" Bert exclaimed. "That's the props building, where they make the scenery for the TV shows!"

"Inside!" Jimmy ordered the Bobbseys.

He nudged them toward the entrance marked *Employees Only*. Except for a row of overhead lights that shone over a long work table, the room was in total darkness. A couple of men were opening boxes in one corner.

"Stack them on the table," one workman ordered the other.

"You stay put," Slim told Bert and Nan, "while we check this stuff out."

"Yeah," Jimmy commented. "Don't try anything stupid—like running away! 'Course I don't think you could get too far on that foot."

Nan leaned against Bert while the pair helped load the boxes on top of each other.

"How much is in them?" Slim asked one of the workers.

"You'll have to count every one."

"We don't have much time," Jimmy said. "I talked to Pester a few minutes ago. He's got the other kids. We're going to meet at the airfield."

"Pester's got Freddie and Flossie!" Nan said.

Bert's mind was racing. Where was Marcy? Were they going to be flown somewhere?

"You!" one of the workmen shouted to Bert. "Come over here! You can help us!"

He directed the boy to an open box. "That's all play money, and I want you to count every piece of it. Understand?"

"Yes, but why?"

"Just do as I say."

"It looks real," Bert observed.

Slim Willis, who was standing near him, beamed. "That's why we have to know how much there is. We are going to pack it on top of the good bills. But there's always a chance some of the fake ones could slip to the bottom and mix with the real stuff."

"Is that how you plan to smuggle the stolen money out of the country?" Bert asked. "By shipping it under the guise of studio props?"

"Smart kid," Sam said. "It was my idea to do it this way."

"Was it also your idea to use studio trucks to carry the money stolen from the San Francisco banks down here?"

The man squinted narrowly at the boy detective, saying, "You ask too many questions. Just count."

Meanwhile, Nan was studying the room. There were small windows, which she could squeeze through, but they were too high to reach. In the back of the room was a door. It was slightly open.

"Nobody's paying attention to me," she said to herself. "Maybe I can sneak out."

Slowly she edged along the wall, pausing when Jimmy looked up from the pile of boxes.

"Going somewhere, little lady?" he asked.

"My foot's kind of stiff. I'm exercising it."

"Just so long as you don't exercise it in the wrong direction," he said, fingering a stack of play money in front of Bert.

Bert shot Nan a warning glance. She nodded at the back door. Bert shook his head, no. He finished counting the money in one box while Slim and Jimmy went through the others. Nan looked on but made no further attempts to escape.

In less than an hour she and her brother were being driven to a clearing on the back lot of the studio. There, on a short runway, sat a small plane ready for take-off. Freddie and Flossie were being led up into it by Edith Willis!

"Freddie! Flossie!" Nan and Bert cried as they emerged from the truck.

The younger twins turned toward their brother and sister. They pushed past Mrs. Willis and dashed to Nan and Bert.

"Oh, Nan!" Flossie wept. "They're going to send us all far, far away. We'll never see Mommy and Daddy again!"

"Now, Floss," Nan tried to comfort her. "Everything's going to be all right."

"No, it isn't," Freddie put in.

Bert put his hand on the boy's shoulder. "Listen—"

"You're supposed to keep an eye on them," Slim shouted to his wife.

But she could barely hear him over the drone of the plane's engine. "I did everything but chain 'em to the ground!" she exploded.

Slim threw up his hands in disgust and marched the Bobbseys back to the plane. "Where are you taking us?"

"Let's say you're going to take a trip to never-never land," he replied. "You'll be flying around while we pack our bags for Mexico!"

"Not me!" Freddie exclaimed.

Like lightning, he broke away from Slim and darted toward the surrounding trees.

"Come back here, you little twirp!" Slim yelled.

"Run, Freddie, run!" Bert cried.

"Get him, Jimmy!" Slim shouted.

Jimmy leaped into his truck and whizzed after him. The small boy darted up a low cliff. Angrily, Jimmy tried to follow him. He revved the engine hard. The truck's wheels spun in the dirt. The vehicle started up the slope but finally backed down. Freddie had completely disappeared from view.

"Don't lose him!" Slim exclaimed.

Like lightning, Freddie broke away from Slim!

"I can't get this truck up the hill!" Jimmy called in reply.

At this moment, Pester Davis stepped out of the little plane and motioned to Edith Willis. "It's all set."

"The other boy's gone!" she told Pester, running toward him.

"Well, get him!"

"We can't. He went over that cliff. Jimmy isn't able—"

"We can't afford to lose any more time over these kids," he stated. "Slim, we'll head for your house after we pick up Edith. I want to figure out each one's share before we take off."

Slim and his wife had blocked Nan, Bert, and Flossie, preventing them from running away. Now they forced them up the plane steps. "Move!" Edith Willis ordered them.

"I don't want to—" Flossie began. She tried to slip out of the woman's firm grasp. "I want to go with Freddie!"

"Oh no you don't!" Mrs. Willis replied, pulling Flossie's curls. "I said move!"

"Give us some time to get out of here," Pester said to the woman.

"How far from here should we meet you?" her husband asked.

"On the other side of those trees."

Nan looked at Bert. "What's going on?"

The boy's stomach churned nervously. "I don't know."

"I don't want to know," Flossie mumbled.

One by one the children took seats inside the small twin-engine plane. The outside door was shut and the steps were removed. Edith Willis, wearing a dark-brown leather jacket and brown slacks, sat behind the instrument panel. She waved to her husband and the other men, then rode the plane forward. In seconds it lifted.

The Bobbseys braced themselves as it clipped the tops of the trees at the edge of the clearing. It circled the studio lot once. Bert and Nan looked down at the menacing trio below.

"Are you a stunt lady?" Bert asked Edith Willis.

She looped the plane up and over. "There's your answer." She smiled.

"Are you going to fly all of that money to Mexico?" Flossie asked, feeling the lump in her throat rise.

"Too risky," the woman replied. "Besides, nobody in their wildest dreams would imagine that stolen money would be wrapped up in a box of props. King was pretty smart to work this deal through the studio."

"King? Who's King?" Nan inquired.

"Oh, he's the big man behind us. I never met the man personally but he sure knows us."

"You mean somebody else is running things for

you?" Nan went on, hoping the woman would reveal the whole story.

"Not exactly. You see King knows all about Slim and me—our police records, our connection with Globe Studios. There was no way for us not to do this job for him."

"You were in jail?" Bert asked.

Mrs. Willis became quiet.

"It's too bad you couldn't make an honest living after being in jail," Nan said.

"It's none of your business," Mrs. Willis said. "We did what we had to do. It's just unfortunate that you had to mix into our affairs. If Slim had only had his wits about him, you'd have never found that key—"

The Bobbseys wanted to question the woman further, but she got up from her seat. "You are going to do some sightseeing for a while—" she announced, "before you run out of fuel."

"What?" Flossie said.

"You heard me. I put the plane on automatic. That means you don't need me any longer. I've got an appointment in Mexico City."

She slipped a parachute pack on her back and chucked Flossie under the chin. "You kids are so smart," she said. "There are a couple of chutes stowed on board. You're welcome to join me!"

She grinned at the young detectives, then slid the narrow door open. Wind rushed inside, whipping the children back in their seats.

"Please don't leave us!" Flossie begged.

"Good-byyyyeeee!" the woman exclaimed and jumped from the plane.

As Edith Willis floated down, Nan and Bert slid the door back into place. "What are we going to do?" each wondered anxiously.

They stared through the small windows at the stars twinkling in the distance. Neither spoke while the plane droned through space.

CHAPTER XVIII

STAR RESCUE

As Bert and Nan listened to the steady moan of the plane's engine, Flossie noticed something orange sticking out of a compartment next to her. It was a piece of canvas. She tugged on it.

"That's a parachute!" Bert exclaimed, excited.

"Are there any others?" Nan asked.

"I'm looking," her brother said. He was on his knees, digging through the material. "There's one, two—" he said.

"Oh, please find another one," Nan hoped.

"No, that's all."

Nan lowered her eyes sadly. "You go. I'll—I'll stay behind." She gulped bravely.

"You're going, too," Bert declared.

"But how?"

"You put this pack on," he told his sister. "Flossie and I will jump together."

"You can't do that!" Nan said. "Please."

"Are you trying to tell your older brother what to do?" he laughed.

For the first time in the past few hours Nan's face broke into a smile. "Older by five minutes," she said.

"Are we going to jump—really jump?" Flossie questioned.

She gazed at the terrain below. They had flown past the clearing and trees and were approaching another open field.

"But it's dark down there," Flossie went on. "I see a couple of lights over in those trees but that's all. Oh, I'm scared. I don't want to jump."

"We're not leaving you behind," Bert said.

He slipped the parachute pack on his back and adjusted the straps to fit around Flossie. Fearfully, Nan watched him.

"That'll never hold both of you, Bert," she said.

"It will have to."

He gave Nan instructions about opening the parachute as he inspected her harness. "See this ring?"

"Mm-hmm."

"Pull it. Your chute will open right away."

Nan's legs felt like rubber as she and her twin

brother pushed the door back, letting the wind ripple across their faces.

"All set?" Bert asked.

Nan said yes.

"Go!" Bert cried.

She pinched her eyes shut and said a prayer. In an instant, she leaped into space and floated downward. Bert, hugging Flossie close to him, followed. Her tiny body shivered as they swayed gently through the air. Bert glanced below.

"Oh, no!" He gasped.

He had misjudged where they would land. The wind blew the children toward a small cluster of lights focused on a clearing edged with tall, thick trees. They drifted in front of the lights.

"Cut!" a voice called out. "What—"

It was John Kordel. Bert and Flossie settled on the ground within a few yards of their sister. As quickly as he could, Bert untied himself and stumbled toward Nan.

"Are you all right?"

She nodded shakily as the crewmen emerged from behind cameras. "What happened? What happened?" several of them asked.

Nan got to her feet weakly and collapsed against the director. Briefly Bert related all that had occurred that evening. Flossie, in the meantime, was trying to untangle herself from the parachute harness.

"Oh, no!" Bert gasped.

"Let me help you with that, honey," Abe Haberman offered.

"Oh, Mr. Haberaber," Flossie mumbled. "I'm so happy to see you!"

She gave the man a big kiss as a large sheep dog bounded toward. "Cheesecake!" she exclaimed, cuddling him.

"Don't you know that's Waldo?" Mr. Kordel smiled. "He strolled into the studio—practically walked up to me and shook my hand. He's a little easier than Cheesecake to work with so I'm glad he can do this scene for me."

"Say, where's Freddie?" the make-up man inquired. "He's not still up there, I hope." He glanced up.

"We've got to go out to the airfield," Bert said.

"You mean the one here on the lot?" the director asked.

"Yes."

"That's where Freddie is. At least, I hope so," Bert said.

"I'm going too," Nan declared, limping on her weak foot.

"Me too," Flossie insisted.

"Okay," Mr. Kordel said. "We'll take the jeep. Wayne, please call security and ask them to meet us out there."

Wayne Little immediately clicked on his walkie-talkie and relayed the message. Before he finished speaking, the Bobbseys and the director were on their way. When they arrived at the airfield, it was deserted.

"They're all gone," Nan commented.

"Probably in Mexico by now," Bert added.

"And maybe with Freddie," Flossie remarked.

"If it's any comfort to you kids," Mr. Kordel began, "they couldn't possibly have reached the California-Mexican border yet. Based on what you've told me, I'd say they haven't even gotten to San Diego yet."

Suddenly Flossie's eyes fell on the shadow of a figure in a distant tree. She blinked twice. "Look over there!" she exclaimed, pointing.

The others followed the line of her finger. "Somebody's caught in those branches," Bert said.

As they drew nearer, they heard the faint plea for help.

"It's Mrs. Willis!" Nan cried.

"Help!" the woman begged louder. "Please get me out of this tree!"

"Just a minute, Mrs. Willis," Bert called up to her quietly.

"Why, it's you!" she said in surprise. "But how did you—you couldn't have—I mean, no one could have—"

"Oh, but we did," Nan said happily, "thanks to my older brother."

Mrs. Willis, whose harness had snagged on a

sturdy limb, flapped her arms and legs. "I'll get you—I'll get you!" she said.

"You'll have to deal with more than these children, Edith," John Kordel said.

The woman grumbled under her breath and stopped kicking. "Oh, it's all Slim's fault."

As she spoke, a rescue truck pulled onto the field. Freddie popped out of it and flew to his brother and sisters.

"Freddie, Freddie!" Flossie squealed. "You're all right."

"Oh, sure," he replied. "I sneaked past Slim."

"Humph!" Edith Willis interrupted.

"As I said," Freddie went on, "I managed to hide long enough. They gave up looking for me. Boy, was I glad. I ran all the way to the front lot and you know what?"

"What?" Nan asked.

"Nobody would believe me when I told them that you were flying in a plane without a pilot and that—" The boy gulped, out of breath. "I saw Mrs. Willis jump—"

"Just take it easy," Mr. Kordel said. "You can tell us all about it later."

The rescue truck, in the meantime, had set a ladder against the tree trunk where Edith Willis hung helplessly. A studio car joined the group as the woman was lowered to the ground.

"I'll fix you," she glared at the Bobbseys.

Bert revealed her connection with the San

Francisco bank robberies. "It was a very clever plot," he told the officers and pulled out one of the photos that they had turned in to the local police.

"A friend of ours found a roll of film—" Nan started to say, suddenly realizing that Marcy Sigler was still missing. "Freddie, what happened to Marcy?" she asked.

"I don't know. We went to check the shed behind the Willis house while Marcy rang the front door. Next thing we knew Mrs. Willis here was right behind us."

The young detectives gazed at the woman. "Where is she?" Mr. Kordel questioned.

She set her jaw firmly and refused to answer.

"You know, Mrs. Willis, it will not help your case one bit if you don't cooperate."

"I'm not talking."

"Is Marcy at the house?" Flossie asked.

The woman breathed hard and turned her face away.

"Is she?" Bert asked.

"Maybe we ought to drive out there," Mr. Kordel said.

"We're always slowing down your production," Bert said.

The director sighed. "I'm getting used to it. As a matter of fact, I'm amazed I've gotten as much of the script done as I have," he said, as he headed back to the area where he had been filming.

"Wayne will have to sub for me while we go out to the Willises. We've been taking **P.O.V.** shots for your night scene."

"P.O.V.?" Freddie repeated, puzzled.

"Point of view," Mr. Kordel explained. "We're filming the terrain from different angles. After we shoot your scene with you in it, we'll match in some of this other film."

Without explaining to the rest of the crew, he left the studio. The drive through the canyon and up the coastal highway seemed unending. When they finally reached the Willis home, it was completely dark. Even the street light in front of it had been broken. The group ascended the porch steps and tried the door. It was locked.

"Let's go around to the back," Bert said. "Those men went in and out of the house that way, mostly."

"This is better than a TV show!" Mr. Kordel quipped.

Bert motioned everyone to be still. "Listen!" he whispered, climbing the back stairway.

"Somebody's in there!" Nan cried.

She jiggled the doorknob. It did not budge.

"One, two, three," Mr. Kordel said, motioning everybody to push against the door at once.

Instantly, it flung wide open. Inside on the floor by the stove was Marcy! She was bound and gagged. Quickly, the Bobbseys and their companion tore the rope and cloth off her mouth, hands, and feet.

"I was beginning to think no one would ever find me," she said, clinging to the children.

"You're supposed to chaperone them." The director smiled.

"I know. I'm sorry."

The girls put their arms around the young woman. "At least you're okay," Nan said.

The Bobbseys brought her up-to-date on their evening. "That awful, awful woman Edith Willis," Marcy said. "She ought to be hanged."

"She was." Bert beamed.

"Was she?" Marcy asked in amazement.

Flossie explained how they had been forced into a plane and how Mrs. Willis had gotten trapped in a tree. Marcy laughed.

"Now what, Kord?" she asked.

"These kids have had a rough night and so have you. I suggest you all go back to your hotel. I'm going to tell the police everything. Bert, on second thought, would you mind coming down to the station with me?"

"I think we all ought to."

The young detectives and Marcy reported what they knew about the stolen money and the set-up.

"Apparently, after the banks were robbed, the money was carried on a Globe Studios truck to Slim Willis's house. It was counted there," Bert said. "Then Slim and his cohorts would pack it under play money he took from the props building and send it along with other studio props, probably, to some movie location in Mexico or maybe Canada."

The next morning, Slim Willis, Jimmy, and Pester Davis were picked up in the Globe City Studios truck. It was heading south for the Mexican border. After the men were booked at the Globe City jail, the twins asked them a few questions.

"Who is Mr. King?" Nan inquired first.

Neither man replied.

"I'll tell you," Slim said finally. "I've got nothing to lose. He's an ex-policeman. He was fired from the Los Angeles force a few years ago. He arrested me one time. After I went on parole, he contacted me. I couldn't figure out how he knew where I was. Of course, I was seeing a parole officer regularly, and I guess he found me through him. Anyway, he said he could get me into real trouble—make me lose my job if I didn't play along with him."

"That's terrible," Bert said.

"Well, I didn't think I had much of a choice. He said he had rigged up this terrific plan for all of us. I thought it was foolproof. Pester and Jimmy said it must be if King dreamed it up. They've got records too."

"Keep quiet," Pester interrupted. "Now you're going to get us into more hot water."

"That's not true," Nan said. "If you tell everything to the police, it might help you."

"Oh, sure, sure. Listen, guys, Miss Detective Bobbsey here will tell you how to shorten your jail terms."

"Nobody asked you for any opinions," Slim snapped at the man. "Look, the kid wants to know. And King isn't going to help us one bit."

"Is that his real name?" Flossie asked.

"No, but since he's the big deal in this whole operation we call him that. His name is Gary Clark."

"Where is he now?"

"I couldn't tell you."

"That's right," Pester finally spoke. "We have no idea where Gary is."

"The police will find him," Nan interjected.

"They'll never catch him—"

"Well, when do you see him?" Bert cut in.

"We don't."

"I don't understand," Flossie said.

"It's very simple," Pester said. "Gary doesn't want to have any personal contact with us. He decided which banks were to be hit. He cased the ones in San Francisco, drew up the plans for them, and deposited them in the L.A. airport locker."

"And sent the key to you on Waldo," Bert finished.

"Yeah."

"Why didn't he just mail you the key?" Nan inquired.

"Because he didn't trust the mail. Gary doesn't live in California—at least I don't think so. He knew he could be sure the dog would reach us faster than a letter and at a definite time. You know, we studio people work on very tight schedules."

"You couldn't let your work slip, could you?" Bert said. "Or make anybody suspicious?"

Slim nodded. "And if I hadn't mixed Waldo up with another dog you would never have found that key and gotten suspicious. We always have doubles of every dog we supply to a show. By the time I realized I had sent Kord the wrong dog, he was gone.

"When you showed me that key at the house, I did my best not to look surprised. I recognized the number on it the minute I saw it. Jimmy and I went through your hotel rooms looking for it." Of course, we didn't find it. But Jimmy said that we could ask security to open the locker for us."

"Leave me out of this!" Jimmy boomed.

Slim went on without glancing at the man. "When I saw Bert drop it in the airport I made a fast dive for it."

"Speaking of falling objects," Nan began, "which one of you loosened that beam on Stage Twenty-four?"

None of the men spoke.

"I know one of you must have. I saw you."

"You didn't see us, kiddo."

"Well, one of you drove us out in a dressing-room trailer to a cliff on the back lot. You tried to strand us."

"Not us," Slim said.

The Bobbseys were perplexed. The next few days found them puzzling over these unanswered questions. On the final day of filming Grady Potts appeared on the set with Caramel and Chester.

"My brother and sister have been signed to be in the next episode of this series," Grady told the twins. "And I just want to thank you."

"For what?" Nan said.

"For bowing out of the next show. The producers told me they wanted you to star in it, but you said you couldn't."

"We have to go home," Bert replied. "We'll be on call for a few guest appearances later. But we have other mysteries to solve."

Grady took a deep gulp of air. "Well, I just want to apologize for everything. I was teed off because Caramel and Chester lost out to you. I tried to—uh—stop the show—stop production whenever I had the chance."

"Then you took us on that whirlwind trip up the cliff!" Nan exclaimed.

"Yes, but I didn't mean to hurt any of you. I just figured Kord would get tired of wondering where you were all the time."

"And he'd fire us, right?" Bert said.

"Right. That's why I let that beam go and led you down to that tricky old boathouse."

"So you knew I was in the van," Bert continued.

"I'm afraid so. Anyway, I'm sorry."

"We are too," Chester said. "We coaxed Waldo offstage—"

"You did?" the Bobbseys asked, incredulous.

"We just wanted to—" Caramel said.

"Make trouble for us," Nan cut in.

"But we didn't mean for him to run away. We were going to return him later on," Caramel replied.

"He took off and we couldn't stop him," her brother added.

"Well, don't worry about it," Flossie said.

"That's right," interrupted Marcy as she hurried toward the group swinging her camera. "I'd like to take a picture of everybody—all the TV mystery stars—Grady, Chester, Caramel. Kord, you join us too."

When everyone was gathered in front of her, she held up the camera. "Smile!" she instructed as a familiar bark broke in. "Okay, Waldo, you ham, you can be in the picture!"

The fluffy sheep dog pranced up to the Bobbseys with a small silver statue in his mouth.

"Is that for us?" Flossie asked, her eyes widening.

"That's your very own special Emmy award,"

the director announced. "It's from all of the crew to you with love!"

Grinning, Freddie accepted the little statue from Waldo and shook his paw. Before he could say anything, Wayne Little rushed forward.

"Hey, it just came over the news. "The plane you kids jumped from ditched in a nearby canyon. The police just found it," he exclaimed. "And they've caught the mastermind behind those bank robberies!"

"You mean King—Gary Clark?" Nan declared.

"That's him."

"Hooray!" the young detectives chorused happily.

Waldo wagged his tail in excitement and barked.

"He's your biggest fan!" Marcy laughed.